Warrior
Hemlock Hollow
Book Three
by
Sandra Kaye

WARRIOR

First edition. July 29, 2024.

Copyright © 2024 Sandra Kaye.

ISBN: 979-8227157157

Written by Sandra Kaye.

Chapter One

Lewis

Bringing the hellion calling herself Raine Hemlock back to my home with me was the last thing I wanted. I didn't need or want the headache of training a fledgling. But train her I would and if her cravings got the better of her, I'd kill her, as was my duty as her sire. She would not become the monster I once was. The number of people I killed before I learned control was a burden I would forever carry.

I pushed the dark thoughts from my mind and focused on the heavy bag I was punching. I wasn't used to feeling uncertain, but I had felt that way since Esmeralda Arcane asked for a favor. But when the Alpha or Alpha's wife asked, and you owed them, that's precisely what you did.

Yet, from the moment the Witchy-wolf got shot and rose within a matter of only a few heartbeats instead of hours, she started her new life as a Vampire. As a blood-hungry demon. I knew I was in trouble.

It was the seventh day since it had all begun, and there was no way I could continue to put off calling the woman's transition a failure much longer. I didn't know many of my kind, but both Lily and I had talked to everyone we trusted and had found no one who knew of a new vampire taking over forty-eight hours to wake. Nor had they heard of anyone getting right back up after dying, so all I could do was use my best judgment.

"She's making noise, boss," Lily told me as she charged into the gym.

We both raced back to the room. We had been taking turns sitting with her so she wouldn't wake up alone. I didn't want her to hurt herself. New vampires were often angry, overly strong, and confused when they woke.

I her moans greeted me before I was halfway to the room I'd placed her in. She lay on top of the blankets, dressed in nothing but a short top and skimpy bottoms. Her creamy skin was even paler than before her death and glowed like porcelain. Her pale tresses shone in the sunlight streaming through the open courtyard door, and all the blood in my body shot to the wrong head for the current situation.

Chapter Two

Raine

Liam's tongue devoured my mouth while his hands caressed my breasts. His hands drove me crazy as he pinched my taunt nipples. Keeping me on that razor's edge between pleasure and pain. Lucian, not one to be outdone, lapped my pussy with his skilled tongue. Liam swallowed my moans as I climbed that orgasmic mountain, begging to reach that blissful peak.

My pleasure built, but as I crested that cliff my body exploded, not in pleasure but in complete and utter pain. Unbearable pain licked through every nerve. Every fiber of my being was on fire. The heat built and built as I continued to fight for every breath through the searing agony.

As I fought past the fog of agony for one wild, dizzying moment, I feared I'd never left my human cage—that this was all something I'd dreamt up to make myself into someone special. That it was a virtual escape for a broken mind. Maybe to some, I appeared weak from all I'd been through. There was a part of me that wondered why I had allowed it to happen at all, but the truth was, I had been young, and I'd believed what we had was love. The way I was treated wasn't my fault; it wasn't my fault. It had taken me a long time to come to terms with that fact, but I knew in my heart it was true. The one thing that the nightmare had done was make me strong. I was a survivor. If I could survive my ex and everything he had put me through, I could survive whatever came next.

My eyes flew open, finally breaking free of the nearly paralyzing pain and fear taking in my surroundings. I was on a large bed with soft pillows and silky sheets. I took stock as I lay there, trying to get my bearings. The door opened, scaring the ever-loving shit out of me, and I bolted from the bed in a flash of movement I wouldn't previously have been capable of. It would have been a kick-ass move if it weren't for the dismount, if you will. My legs tangled in the sheets, and I ended up sprawled on the carpet wearing nothing but a tiny top and barely there panties that did not belong to me.

A pair of bare feet near my face distracted me from the panty situation. I followed the masculine legs up to a tiny pair of dark gray workout shorts that left very little to the imagination. Lewis, the Vampire Demon-Fae or Fae-Demon, as he preferred, looked down at me with his arms crossed over a tattooed chest that was more defined than his suit had hinted at. A fine layer of sweat covered his dark skin. He offered me a hand, but I slapped it away and I untangled myself from the sheets before climbing to my feet while tugging the microscopic shirt down to cover myself.

"How are you feeling?" he asked, watching me closely.

"I'm fine," I snapped.

Being stuck with the Vampire was a sore subject. Lewis and I had only met after my wolf mate's mother gave me his blood before I entered the arena to battle my ex-friend to the death. She had unreciprocated feelings for my wolf mate and wanted to take my place as witch queen. It's a lot I know. While I had won the battle, she shot me a couple times, which apparently would have been fatal if not for my mother-in-law's forethought.

So now I was in a fae realm transitioning into a Vampire-demon while also losing my recently discovered Witch and Wolf sides. To make said transition, I was stuck with the overly attractive Fae-Demon, while my two mates were attempting to manage the fallout from the battle with my false friend.

"Good, I was just heading to breakfast. Why don't you join me? There's much to talk about." he turned and walked through an archway, not waiting for me to reply, just assuming I would follow.

The breakfast part was something I wasn't sure I was up for. I still wasn't certain I was going to drink blood, but answers, those I wanted very much. I didn't, however, want to go traipsing around in borrowed panties and a barely there top. So, I did what any self-respecting woman would do. I fashioned a toga out of the bedsheet and strutted after my jailer.

Visitors accessed the paved courtyard through the archway, which was surrounded by walkways with marbled stone pillars at intervals along the space. Nearby, the open area revealed the second floor and walkway. The sun was shining; the sky was clear blue, and there was a slight breeze that carried the scent of jasmine, roses and lilac. It was the hypnotic aroma that captivated me. Lewis sat at a table for two in the center of the courtyard, near a large tree that sprouted from the ground. The tiles formed a bench seat around it. Lewis sat on one side in the tree's shade. I took the chair across from him and was pleased to see fruit, yogurt, bagels, and orange juice instead of blood. It wasn't until I'd finished making myself a plate and had taken several bites of my bagel that I realized I'd just walked through the sun to get to the table. I didn't know a great deal of facts about vampires, but I knew they couldn't go out in the sun and that they did indeed drink blood.

"Is this some type of illusion or something?" I asked, motioning to the sky with my bagel.

"No." One word, that's all I got as he tossed grapes into his mouth and chewed. The whole time he stared at me with his odd red eyes.

"Care to explain?" I snarled, suddenly very angry.

"Not really, but I doubt you are the type to stop asking, so I guess I must. This is just as it seems-."

"But vampires can't go out into the sun," I interrupted, gawking at my arm where a ray of sunshine was touching my skin. Not understanding how we weren't bursting into flames. "Or are we like that one where vampires sparkle in the sun?" I asked, moving my arm back and forth, checking for sparkles. There weren't any. I must admit, I felt disappointed.

"Correct. Normal vampires cannot go out in direct sunlight without being very uncomfortable. They don't burst into flames or anything as portrayed in your movies and books. Nor do they sparkle. I, however, do not have an aversion to sunlight. Likely because of my dual nature. Which is helpful since I'm also a light fae and light fae need sunlight to rejuvenate our cells. This makes us nearly immortal," he explained.

"So, I inherited your ability to day-walk?"

"It would appear so," he admitted, as he tossed another grape into his mouth.

"Wait? You didn't know?" I shrieked, bolting to my feet, knocking over the chair and tipping the table, sending our drinks and food flying in the process.

"I did not."

"Thanks, you jerk. What was your plan exactly? Wait for the sun to kill me so you wouldn't have to deal with me?" I snarled.

"It would not have killed you. It would have merely stung a bit," he told me nonchalantly.

I tossed a fireball as I spun and stomped back toward the room, where I'd woken.

His laughter followed me, making me wish I'd aimed for his head. But since that small flame had sapped my strength, I slammed the bathroom door instead, blocking out his laughter.

Chapter Three

Lewis

Lily must have heard the commotion because she arrived moments after my guest stormed back to her room. Lily is a young fire mage, and she's been with me since she was about ten years old. When I found her, she was living on the streets of Chicago. She had no one. She didn't even have a name. I found her when I was there hunting a vamp who had been slaughtering humans and supernaturals. I'd hunted him across four states before I finally cornered him. He'd made the unfortunate decision to use the girl as a hostage. Vampires burn just like anyone else. She lit him on fire and ran screaming into my arms. She had no clue of the danger I could pose to her. As her tiny body shook, she clung to me. Whether it was because of the cold or fear, I could not be sure.

I couldn't bear to leave her there in the cold, so I brought her home. She picked her name, and her birthday became the day we met. She was more than the help. I considered her as my daughter. We started as just two strangers, but now we were family.

"I see you are already winning her over with your charming personality," Lily teased.

"One of my many gifts," I quipped.

She chuckled and shook her head, "What's that the humans say? Something about catching bees and honey."

"I don't wish to catch bees nor anything else. I just want to get her through her transition and be done with her."

"You should be nicer to her. She's been through a great deal in a short span of time," she reminded me as she worked.

Bringing Lucian Arcane's new mate back to my personal realm was the last thing I thought I'd be doing when his mother asked for my blood. Not that I could have refused, even if I had wanted to. Her father was there for me when no one else was. I would do anything for him and, by extension, his daughter. Though truthfully, I hadn't feared the hybrid might die. She was the only known hybrid born with the ability to fully use both sides of her heritage, even after living as a human for nearly forty years, and she would not have if the power-hungry witch she was battling hadn't resorted to the weapons of humans. It was one of the rare things all supernatural as a whole agreed on. We thought it was beneath us to use guns. Yet it was a bullet to the heart that had brought the hardheaded beauty into my life.

With her pale tresses, large soulful eyes, and full lips, she was a distraction I didn't have time for. Everything about her appealed to me and having her near was painful. Watching her grief as she lost the powers she was born to yield touched a part of me I thought long dead.

She didn't want to be a bloodsucker like me, and I understood that on a level she would never know. I too hated the vampire that bit me and made me what I am now. Before that night, I was a royal fae with little worry what my future held.

Afterwards, I was a shadow of myself, a freak of nature. However, what followed is why I refused to let her suffer the same fate. I may not have wanted to be a sire, but I would not leave her to the same fate. No matter how hard being near her was.

She had been in my home for only a week and awake for mere hours and already I couldn't get her out of my head. I intended to push her buttons to evaluate how well she could manage her emotions. That she only knocked over the table was a pleasant surprise. As was the fact that she had no reaction to the sun. While it's true that Vampires have an aversion to the sun, it's nothing like what books and movies portray. It's uncomfortable and makes them weaker. I've never known why I do not have that weakness. Nor why I could keep some of my powers after my change. I have always assumed that there is a relation between the two, but I could never confirm my belief.

Chapter Four

Raine

After a really, really long shower, I got my temper back under control. Admittedly, it took longer than I would have liked, but along with the sapped magical strength, I'd noticed I was faster, stronger and angered way quicker. Calm didn't come quite as quickly.

Thankfully, Lewis had sent someone with clothes, food and a note saying to join him in the gym when I was ready. I knew he had not left because his smell was present in the room and on the note but not on the clothes or on the tray of food. They had a decidedly feminine scent. I'd smelled the same scent in the room, like she had spent time in the room where I'd woke.

My unknown savior had left leggings, a sports bra and new panties, thankfully all with tags still attached. The bacon, eggs, and toast got my attention first. The few bites of bagel I'd managed before storming off had done little to tame the hungry beast residing in my belly. I devoured the food but still could have eaten a great deal more.

After getting dressed and pacing the room for so long, I memorized every corner. I finally gave up waiting for the unknown female and went in search of the gym. Turned out it was easy enough to find. I just followed my nose. I may lose my wolf, but for the moment, my heightened smell was still fully functional. The idea I was losing that part of me when I'd only just found it gutted me. I shook off the thought as I followed the smell of sweat and blood to find Lewis pummeling a heavy bag.

I stood watching him. I had to admit he was a thing of beauty as he danced with the bag. With his long raven hair, chiseled form, and bronze skin etched with tattoos, he was perfect in a pair of basketball shorts. His shorts were so low I could see the V-shape of his hip muscles pointing to the pleasure zone. I found I very much wanted to see more.

I'm not sure how long I stood there before he spoke.

"Are you enjoying the view?" he asked without looking at me.

My face flushed as I ignored his question. "You beckoned, my lord?" I said with a curtsy.

"That was over an hour ago."

"And?" I snapped, walking past him to a mat by the wall and started stretching. While doing my best to ignore his gaze.

He grabbed his shirt from the floor and left the room without a backwards glance.

I tried the punching bag. I'd never tried hitting one. I preferred the sound of flesh, but figured it couldn't be too difficult. It was harder than I thought it'd be, but I eventually got into a rhythm.

The hair on the back of my neck suddenly stood on end as my early warning system kicked in a moment before I sensed movement behind me. I ducked as a fist slammed into the bag at the level my head had just been. I kicked out, attempting to sweep my attacker's legs from under them, but met only air. Dodging a second jab, I landed in a crouch and sprang to my feet.

Lewis' hits were so rapid I had no clue how I dodged as many as I did, but the ones that he landed packed a hell of a punch. We battled until we were both dripping with sweat. When we finally stopped, he tossed me a bottle of water and a hand towel before retrieving both for himself.

I gulped from the bottle. It was ice cold, just the way I liked it. I had downed half the bottle without taking a breath.

"How do you feel?" He asked when I took a breath.

"I'm fine," I told him, sitting down on the floor to catch my breath.

"No edginess? Pain? Fatigue?" He questioned, sitting as well. He seemed more at ease than during our previous encounters.

I nearly told him *no* before truly taking stock. Once I did, I answered as honestly as I could, "Not pain exactly."

"What about after you used your witch powers?" he queried.

"I felt tired and hungry after, but I feel fine now," I admitted.

"The hunger isn't altogether surprising considering you were asleep for seven days-,"

"Seven," I squawked, interrupting him mid-sentence.

"Yes, and fanning that dying witch flame couldn't have been without cost," he informed me matter-of-factly.

I did my best not to strangle him over his callous remark. "So, my powers really are fading?" I asked, praying he was wrong.

"Yes, as I said they would." His tone was flat and without emotion.

It made it all worse somehow.

Raw fury rolled through my veins, and I just couldn't deal with any of it. Not the anger and not the hollow feeling his words caused to bloom in my chest. So, I stood, tossed my water bottle in the recycle bin and stomped back to the room before I clocked him or tried to at any rate. Our sparring had made it plain; he was a very skilled fighter.

Chapter Five

Lewis

I hated that my words hurt her. I remembered the feeling of loss she was currently dealing with. There was nothing I could do for her except be honest. Truthful and direct was the safest way forward. If she wanted comfort, she was stuck with the wrong guy. I'd leave the comfort to her mates.

She had a long hard road ahead of her and if she was going to survive and return to her two mates; I had to train her to deal with the roller coaster ride of emotions that came with transitioning into a new vampire. With the transition came heightened senses. All of them, all at once, not just strength and speed as most people believed, but sight, sound and desire as well.

Vampires felt everything on a level few could tolerate. Less than ten percent lived past the first week. Many because of uncontrolled bloodlust. Mostly because their minds aren't able to deal with the overstimulation. Those of us that endure must deal with what we have become and for those like me, we must also come to terms with what we've done. It was not for the weak of spirit or faint of heart.

I was going to do my best to ensure she didn't have to live with the same nightmares I did. Nor would she spend the rest of her existence trying to make amends. No, she would stay here, isolated from the outside world, until I was sure it was safe for her to return to the human realm. In my realm, I had better control over exposing her to certain people and things. There were limited people who could find my home, let alone enter without my consent. Those who did were all strong enough to protect themselves. Even my staff were well aware of what could go wrong with her and were paid handsomely for their risk. And if for some unfortunate reason I cannot teach her control, then as her sire, it will fall to me to end her. Yet another reason to avoid getting overly friendly with my attractive house guest.

I finished my water and headed back to my room for a quick shower before it was time for my guests' next feeding. So far, she had managed her mood swings admirably, but I didn't want to let her go too long between feedings or that might change quickly.

Though how she could still access her witch powers was an oddity, I needed to understand as soon as possible. She couldn't afford to get her hopes up and while she was still relying on her former magic, she wouldn't be able to fully embrace her new existence.

Chapter Six

Raine

I made it back to my room. It only took three wrong turns and one dead end. To my delight, I found more food and clean clothes. This time a pair of jeans and a T-shirt, again with tags attached. The smell told me it was the same gift fairy as before. Her scent was floral and campfire. Odd, but not unpleasant.

My wolf was ravenous and making itself-known. When I saw the food, the beast in my belly let out a loud growl. Nonetheless, I had worked up a major sweat and wanted to shower again first because my sweat was becoming overwhelming. I stepped into the bathroom, but as I reached to turn on the shower, my internal warning bells started blaring.

The ability was still new to me, so I searched the room for threats. When I found none, I headed back towards the bedroom looking, listening, even smelling for what had set off my radar. A thorough search of the room also found no threat, but my gut continued to tell me there was danger somewhere. I had turned to give the room a second visual pass as a throat clearing had me swinging around to find a strange male watching me from the archway to the courtyard.

"What do we have here?" The stranger asked, stepping into the room uninvited.

"Who are you?" I demanded, watching as the man took another step into my room. "I think that's quite far enough"! Forming a small energy ball, I barked, prepared to fry his ass if he took one more step into my private domain.

"Oh, aren't you a lovely little witch? What exactly is my son doing with the likes of you?" His tone was sleazy, and I didn't care about the way he was looking at me. More leer than look.

Yet another visitor spared me from answering. "Mister Tuatha de Dannan Mister Damon did not mention you would visit," a slip of a girl stood in the doorway to the inner hall. By the scent, I was betting she was the one leaving me with the clothes and food.

I may have recognized her scent, but I still didn't know her, which left me between two unknowns, and I didn't like it. Not one bit. I stepped slowly toward the wall behind me, trying to keep an eye on both of them.

"Lily dear, always a pleasure to see you," the male said. As he spoke, he took another step closer. His words said one thing while her response said something altogether different. Her hunched posture and clenched jaw told me she feared him. My gut told me he knew it and enjoyed it.

That was all I needed to know to choose a side. I growled as I blocked his path to her. He smiled as he took another step closer. Without hesitation, I transformed into my wolf and lunged for his throat before completing my transformation fully. I had teeth and claws and I intended to use them.

My snout, however, slammed into an invisible barrier. I landed on the tile floor dazed as the pale-haired stranger looked down at me. From where I landed, I could see his leafy green eyes.

"Bad dog!" He chastised, walking around my frozen form. "So not *only* a witch, but a shifter as well? What is that boy up to now?" he mused aloud.

If it weren't for the pounding in my head from whatever it was my snout collided with, I would have attempted it a second time after his comment. Since I was still seeing two of him, I opted to wait. At least until I could be sure which one he really was.

"Father enough! Leave her be," Lewis barked. To me he said, "Lily will take you somewhere safe so your wolf can run. Lily, you know where to take her and take some clothes. She will need them when she shifts back."

Lily nodded and gathered the clothes from where I'd left them in the bathroom before standing in the doorway waiting for me.

I looked from Lewis to the girl, then to the intruder, before baring my teeth and growling my disapproval. Then I slowly turned to follow the slip of a girl from the room. She led me through the halls until she reached the kitchen. There was an older woman chopping vegetables as we passed. She looked from my escort to me and returned to her chopping without a word. We continued down several back halls. From the lack of décor and cheap wood doors that were lining the narrow corridors, it was clear this was the servant area. She finally opened the door and stepped through. The smell of honeysuckle and magnolia hung heavy in the air. I crept closer to the threshold. A forest lay before me with large beautiful southern live oaks, complete with Spanish moss. There were magnolia and palmetto trees, as well. If I didn't know any better, I could believe myself still in Georgia. Not as good as Hemlock Hollow, but I had grown to love Georgia and my new wolf family there.

It felt like so long ago that I left my wolf and witch mates. I hated that Lucian and I had spent so much time working against our true mate bond. Him because he was receiving threats on my life if he attempted to complete our bond. Meanwhile, I was being attacked at every turn in the hopes that an injury would give my foe the upper hand. The worst part was that, in the end, it was revealed that the culprits were one and the same. My former friend and witch Theresa Goody.

My wolf and I howled before dashing into the forest. My wolf helped me to distance myself from the fatigue and anger. For a time, I ran, stretching my weary muscles until I found myself back at the door where the woman Lily stood holding a bundle of clothes.

When I didn't immediately shift back, she must have thought I was shy. "I'll just leave these here and wait for you inside if you like?" She must have realized her mistake, because she chuckled as she stepped inside. It was a pleasantly whimsical sort of sound. I liked it.

If I could have replied, I'd have told her my hesitance had nothing to do with being shy and everything to do with the fact I had had little practice shifting.

Chapter Seven

Lewis

Once Lily took Raine away, I was safe to deal with my father. Not that he claimed that title in public. He didn't. I was a blight on the family. He took everything from me, including my name, when he turned me. He labeled me a demon and instead of fighting him; I agreed. From that day forward, I took Damon as my last name. I refused to hide any longer.

"To what do I owe this unwelcome visit, father?" I used the term just to piss him off.

"Always so cranky. If I had as many lovelies at my beck and call as you, I'd never stop smiling," he leered, walking around Raine's room like he owned the place...

"I'm sure you didn't come all this way to inquire as to the company I keep. So again, I ask, what brings you?" I repeated, attempting to keep my temper in check. There weren't many who could cause me to lose my cool, but my father was at the top of that very short list. He had denied me for decades because I was of no use to him. Now it appeared I was again.

"I have a job for your band of misfits," he sneered.

"I've told you before not to call them that!" I barked, letting him see my irritation. "They are my *House*. If you wish for this conversation to continue, you will refer to them as such." My House comprised anyone that did not fit into other supernatural subtypes or those that did not wish to. Being in a house gave them rights they would not have otherwise. I helped them in whatever way I could and in exchange I represented them on the supernatural council. It allowed them to have a vote in laws and such. Before my fledgling crashed into our world, it was the only way the unwanted could have a voice, as well as protection. Being on their own would not.

"Yes, of course. I did not mean to offend. It has been a taxing week," he apologized. "Children are going missing, and I need your trackers to help us find them... Please?" He pleaded.

"Why aren't you using your own royal trackers?"

"Whoever is taking the children is masking their trail from my best fae trackers. I believe they may use dark magic. If that is the case, the children will only live long enough for them to be sacrificed. I do not have the allies I once did. I need your help. "These children are in great danger," he said, his smug tone replaced with fear."

My father did not have very many positive qualities, but he loved his people. Well, the pure ones anyway. And he knew I could never say no if there was a chance I could help. Especially if there were children involved.

"How many children?" I asked.

"Seven so far."

"In what time frame?"

"Seven," was his reply.

"One each day?"

"No. One on the first night, one on the third night, at which time I implemented a curfew. Two more during the fourth day and three last night," he explained.

"During the day?" I inquired.

"Yes, the third child was walking home. She was only three doors away and number four was playing in the backyard. After that, no child was to be outside alone."

"Then, I presume three children got taken while they were out together?"

My father had clearly tried to protect them, but to no avail. We talked for a short time before he left with the agreement that I would send a tracker straight away.

After he left, I was about to send a fire message to Hector when there was a knock at the office door, followed by Natessa.

"Hey uncle. Sorry to just barge in, but I knocked, and no one answered. Not even Lily. I was worrying something was wrong until I spotted that asshat ex father of yours leaving," she told me, plopping down in the chair in front of my desk.

"You know you are always welcome, Natessa. Is this a social call?"

"I wish, but unfortunately no. Have you heard about the missing children?" she asked.

"Unfortunately, yes, my father was just here recruiting our help," I informed her.

"Whoa, really? Since when does he give a shit about anyone but fae?" she huffed.

"He isn't, but he is quite invested because all seven children ended up being fae."

"Well... That explains a lot and makes my visit here even more urgent. The children I was talking about are apparently besides the seven he told you about. I came to tell you about the two children from our house as well as two shifters from rogue families in the area that have gone missing," she explained.

"So, eleven children in total? A mix of supernaturals?"

"That we're aware of, yes. I came to recruit your help and ask to use Hector. The trolls and shifters have had no luck. I attempted it even after Suma was taken. Even her scent was undetectable, and it had only been two hours. Nothing," she informed me. "Now I find out there are fae children missing as well. That can't be a coincidence. Can it?"

Suma was Natessa's ten-year-old niece, and they were very close. That she was as calm as she appeared was a miracle. I knew her well enough to know it was a front.

"I doubt that very much."

Chapter Eight

Raine

Lily came out twice to check on me before I shifted back. It was getting easier each time, but I was still slow compared to Lucian. I hated thinking I was going to lose the ability just as I was understanding it. My legs were shaky as I dressed. Thankfully Lily had a plate heaping with roast beef, mashed potatoes and carrots waiting for me. I loved that she kept bringing me food. Never had I been so hungry before. I consumed two heaping plates and a large piece of the most delicious chocolate cream pie I'd ever eaten. If I continued to eat like I was, I was going to be an overweight vampire very soon. I wondered if that was a valid worry as I contemplated a second slice.

"If you are no longer feel hungry, madam, I could guide you to the study where the monsieur is waiting for you," Lily offered.

Since I planned to demand he let me visit my mates, I followed her. I couldn't believe it had been a week already without seeing, talking to or touching either of my mates.

We exited the kitchen in the opposite direction from which we had entered. The halls that we walked this time were wide and opulent, unlike the corridors she took me through in my wolf form. I still didn't see any people as we walked, though.

It seemed like a rather large home since, other than Lewis and Lily, I'd only seen the cook and his father. From the conversation earlier, it was clear Lewis hadn't expected him, so he clearly didn't live there. That was good, since the thought of him made me see red.

We made our way through the halls to a closed door. The voices coming through the door were familiar, yet it wasn't until I stepped inside and saw her, that it clicked. Tessa Damon, of all people, sat in one of the plush chairs in front of the large desk behind which sat Lewis, aka my jailer.

"What the hell are you doing here?" she demanded.

"I was going to ask you the same damn thing! I thought this was my own personal hell, not yours." I quipped, as I hauled her from the chair and wrapped her in a warm embrace.

She laughed as she returned my hug. Tessa and I weren't as close as some of the other girls in our gang, but she felt like home, so I held on for an extra minute.

"Hell is what you make of it, Chica," she told me good-naturedly, patting my back with only a little of her discomfort showing.

I stuck out my tongue and flipped her off as I plopped down into the second chair, knowing it would ease that discomfort.

"There's the Witch sass I'm used to. I was worried I was going to have to comfort those sexy ass mates of yours." Her smile said it was a joke, but my heart gave a pang. The thought of losing everything I'd just discovered was too much to bear. Losing my wolf, my witch power, and both my mates (even if only temporarily). It left me feeling empty, alone, and furious at the injustice.

She must have noticed my mood change because she laid her hand over mine where it rested on the arm of the chair.

"How are you? How's what was his name, Mark, Markus?" I asked her, changing the subject.

"I'm hanging in. As for Markus, he's out. His man parts kept falling into anything with two sets of lips," she supplied, making me laugh. Truth was Tessa did not date. She had this whole deal with rules and everything. Markus never had a chance at more than hooking up with my girl. If he had, even he wouldn't be stupid enough to cheat unless he wanted to take his life into his own hands.

Lewis stayed silent throughout our exchange, though I could feel his silent gaze and his musky vanilla-sage scent intensified during our chat. Training with the Alpha of Alphas (a.k.a. Lucian's father) had helped me hone my heightened senses. He taught me that everyone had their own unique scent, as did every emotion. His change in smell told me he was feeling something. What I couldn't guess. Not yet anyway.

Lewis was quiet so long I was about to demand answers when he finally spoke. "I see you know each other. That should simplify things."

When he said nothing more, I looked at Tessa whose only response was a one shoulder shrug. I swear the girl could make anything look sexy. With her raven hair, piercing green eyes and killer cheekbones, she was uber attractive. If I swung that way, she'd definitely be my type.

"Simplify what, exactly?" I asked.

"Spending time together, of course," he answered, as if it were obvious.

His minimalistic word shit was getting on my last nerve.

"Why exactly will we be needing to spend time together, uncle?" Tessa asked in her ever-patient tone. She was a lawyer in the human world. It always amazed me how calm she could be when dealing with pain in the ass men. I witnessed her brilliance firsthand when my ex-husband tried to claim half my witch inheritance in our divorce.

"She is transitioning, so she must be near me, or she will suffer great pain. Hector is a skilled tracker, but even he cannot be in two places at the same time... To help you, I need you to show me each place where the abductions took place. With the number of children already missing, there's no guarantee when or if I'll be able to return. As safe as you are here, it just makes sense for you to be with us. If I can't pick up anything and Hector does, we will reach out to another air witch. Time is of the utmost importance. They may be supernatural children, but they are children nonetheless, and we need to find them as soon as possible."

"Wait, children? What children?" I demanded.

Tessa was the one to answer, "There are several children missing."

"I'm not an air witch but I do still have access to my powers, plus my olfactory senses aren't too shabby," I offered, wanting to help but also just to feel useful.

"That won't be necessary," Lewis declared in a dismissive tone.

Chapter Nine

Lewis

My words clearly hurt her feelings, which was never my intention. I had no clue why she could still shift and use her powers. Nothing about her changing had followed a natural course. Most transitioning vampires wake one to three days after death and lose any primary powers within the first forty-eight hours after that. I had woken twenty-seven hours after my first death. Twenty-four hours later, my power had significantly diminished. The fact that they stayed there was unheard of.

Someone shot Raine in the heart. She died and resurrected within minutes instead of hours or days. Then she went into stasis for seven very long days. During which I spent every spare moment staring at her, still waiting and wondering if I'd done something wrong. As much as I knew what would be required,

I was not sure I had it in me. She was more than just a pretty face. Though she was quite lovely as well. It was her strength and hardheaded nature that intrigued me.

I knew very little of her history, but it was clear she had come through it as a strong and capable woman. Which is the only reason I would risk taking her out into the world so soon. Of course, the true test would come when she got to see her mates in person for the first time. Passion and anger were two of the hardest emotions for a new vampire to deal with. Hurting someone you are angry at isn't difficult to process for many. Hurting someone during a passionate moment could be devastating, especially for someone with the level of empathy that she possessed.

She would never feel that soul destroying pain if I had anything to say about the matter.

"So, if I'm so useless in this endeavor? Why can't I just go back to Hemlock House with my mates while you go handle *things*?" she demanded, tapping her foot and crossing her arms under her ample breast while scowling.

"We have already been over this; it is not safe."

"But it's perfectly fine to take me out into the world and risk me attacking someone there?" she demanded.

She was just too damn adorable.

"Besides, my mates are quite capable of protecting themselves and our people. Even from me if need be. They would never allow me to harm one of my citizens," she seethed.

She wasn't wrong about her mates being strong. They were. While I hadn't previously met Liam, he was clearly a very capable witch. Lucian, on the other hand, I knew well. Although since they also loved her, I'd bet they would never hurt her. Not even to protect themselves. If she were my mate, I damn sure couldn't.

"The answer is no. Now I suggest you pack quickly. The longer we wait, the less chance we have of tracking the children. I'm sure you don't want those poor children to suffer just so you can continue to argue. Correct?"

Chapter Ten

Raine

"Ugh..." I growled, stomping out of the office.

He was such a pain in the ass. I freaking hated that he was right. I wanted nothing to happen to those children. Children were sacred in my book and people who harmed them deserved their own special place in hell. Not that I would admit that to him. Especially while I was still angry.

I stormed back to my room, realizing I had nothing to pack. Lily had been bringing me clothes. So other than the clothes on my back, the sweaty workout clothes I could smell all the way across the room and the micro shirt and underwear I woke in, there was nothing to pack.

A tap at the door pulled me from my musings. I turned to find the girl I now knew was Lily, standing in the doorway with a large black backpack with hot pink trim and a smaller insulated bag that matched. From the smell, I was sure the smaller bag held food. Ham, wheat bread and pickles and something sweet that had my mouth watering.

"Come on in."

"I brought you everything you might need for your trip and a snack in case you get hungry," she explained, offering me the two bags with a kind smile.

"Thank you so very much," I gushed, sneaking a look into the smaller bag. There were three sandwiches, a large dill pickle, carrots, celery and a small canteen which was where the sweet smell was permeating from. "What's in here?" I asked, pulling it from the bag and unscrewing the lid. It smelled so amazing. I had it to my lips before she could even reply.

"Mr. Damon's blood, ma'am," she informed me, matter-of-factly.

I almost spit it out, but it tasted so amazing I just couldn't. It was like dark chocolate and a medium rare steak all in one. Which should have been awful, yet somehow it wasn't. I drank every drop and still couldn't feel as grossed out as I knew I should be.

There was a warmth that spread from my gut throughout my entire body. It was the most euphoric thing I'd ever felt. Well, short of the knee buckling orgasms my mates could give. Suddenly, I found myself transported from the room back to Lewis' office. It was clear that I wasn't there physically. I could feel my toes in the plush carpet of the room rather than the stone tile I could see lining the office floor. I'd been in a moment before. He was still at his desk and Tessa was still in the chair in front of his desk, as they'd been when I stomped out.

"If I could give you a bit of advice regarding Raine?" Tessa asked.

"Speak your mind, Natessa," he told her.

"Raine has been through a lot in her short life. While it's not my place to decide who knows her story, I can tell you she doesn't do well with commands. She's had enough commanding men to last her immortal lifetime. That being said, she's very level-headed. That's what makes her such a good leader. Well, that and her kind heart." Her words were so unexpected that I gasped.

When I did, my consciousness slammed back into my body. Bringing with it a wave of nausea that had me dropping to my knees while trying not to barf all the delectable blood I'd just drank. Definitely words I never thought to utter.

"Ma'am...Ma'am...?" Lily's hand was on my shoulder, shaking me.

When I finally opened my eyes and looked at her, she looked terrified.

"Should I go get monsieur?" she demanded.

"I'm okay," I finally managed.

"Oh, thank goodness," she huffed, dropping to sit next to me, "You scared the daylights out of me. What happened? If you don't mind me asking?"

The nausea was passing, but I wasn't quite ready to stand up, so I slid off the bed and sat down next to her.

"I honestly don't know. One minute I was downing blood like it was a chocolate milkshake, the next I'm back in the office watching Lewis and Tessa talk about me."

"You have far sight. That is a very rare gift for a vampire," she told me in a reverent tone.

"Well, my head feels like someone hit me between the eyes with a hatchet while his buddy tries his best to remove my head. I don't recommend it," I deadpanned.

She giggled in a melodic tone before telling me, "You're funny."

"Thanks," I muttered while attempting to stand up.

I wobbled, and she offered me a hand. I wasn't sure I needed it, but it was sweet of her, so I took it.

Chapter Eleven

Lewis

Natessa and I sat in silence for a few moments after Raine stormed out of the room. Every time I upset her, it killed me. I hated that she had to be with me when she wanted to be with someone else.

"If I could give you a bit of advice regarding Raine?" Natessa's words pulled me from my musings.

"Speak your mind, Natessa," I told her, suddenly exhausted.

"Raine has been through a lot in her short life. While it's not my place to decide who knows her story, I can tell you she doesn't do well with commands. She's had enough commanding men to last her entire immortal lifetime. That being said, she's very level-headed and down to earth. That's what makes her such a good leader. Well, that and her kind heart. But most of all, she's understanding," she informed me.

I was silent for a few beats, attempting to decipher her meaning without success. "I'm afraid I don't get your drift, as they say."

"Okay, wiseass," she smirked. "Just give her the lowdown on why she can't go home until after she has completed her transition. I know you're worried, but even if you don't tell her about your experience, she needs to know the risk she could pose to her mates and her people and she will do what you need her to. Also, not to tell you how to handle this hunt for the missing children, but Raine has a great deal of power and raw talent hasn't failed her yet."

It was clear Natessa had become friends with my fledgling, but she clearly also admired her. Which wasn't something I'd often heard from her. Natessa was nearly a century old and a member of our house council. She referred to me as uncle, but our relationship was based on choice rather than blood. I valued her opinion as both. I knew she'd understand if I explained how I feared that I had done something wrong in allowing Esmeralda to give her my blood. No one knew what a hybrid like her would be after a change. There had been none in centuries, as far as I was aware. I'll admit I should have asked more questions. I'd heard about the Hemlock heir being discovered and about the witch-wolf hybrid. However, I had no clue until the challenge at the wolf mating games that they were one and the same.

"I can't promise that I can always stop and explain. Is it not better to keep the lines clear between sire and fledgling?" I finally asked.

"Hasn't that already happened?" she asked rather than answer.

Thankfully, a throat clearing saved me from answering. Hector stood in the open doorway.

"Hey Boss, Tessa... Lily said you needed me for something," Hector explained, stepping in and dropping into the chair Raine had vacated.

Hector was a tall, willowy man with dark skin and deep green eyes. Lily and he had grown up together. His mother was human, and she passed from some type of female cancer when he was only nine. She'd been gone only a few months when I brought Lily to live with me. She was wild, and he was angry. Together, his father and I raised them to be strong. His father died three years ago in an attack. He took it hard. I did my best to help him, but it was Lily who reached him with her pure heart and no-nonsense attitude. He was nearly back to the man his father raised. His father and I may not have been born brothers, but that's what we became.

Chapter Twelve

Raine

Turns out standing up wasn't as easy as I thought. If Lily hadn't been holding my arm, I'd have landed flat on my ass for a second time. She helped me to the bed and fetched a cool cloth for my head. After a few minutes, the pain in my head dulled to a tolerable level, so I tried to sit up again. The room spun for a beat, but after I focused on a spot on the wall across from the bed, it slowed to a stop. The wallpaper had vines with small blue flowers. I picked a flower and took slow, deep breaths until my head cleared.

A new power wasn't really something I was looking for. Especially not one that left my head feeling like it'd been through a blender. Nor could I think of anything good that could come from listening in on private conversations.

Not that I wasn't wondering what kind of response Lewis might have made. Knowing him, he hadn't given one. Unless, of course, I was the only one he didn't like to answer.

Tessa's voice, along with a male voice I didn't know, shook me from my musings.

"Are you taking a nap or what girl?" Tessa demanded, crossing her arms under her breast as she tapped her foot.

A tall, slim, dark-skinned man stood behind her, talking to Lily. He was nearly a foot taller than her. Lily wore a wide smile as she chatted animatedly with him in inaudible whispers. It was clear she liked him.

"A girl gotta get her beauty sleep," I joked, climbing to my feet. "Are we heading out?" I asked.

"Yeah, as soon as you're ready to go."

"I'm ready," I informed her, grabbing my lunch and my bag. "Who's the new guy?" I asked, nodding my head in his direction.

"That's Hector. He's the tracker we were talking about. The air witch," she explained. "Lily and Hector are heading to the Fae realm while we head to Damon Cove, where the last child was taken."

"Cool. Let's go." I was nervous she'd know what I overheard. I didn't want to hide it from her, but I wasn't quite ready to admit that the whole situation might have freaked me out a bit. Tessa was a friend, but she wasn't like Becca or Olivia. They always wanted to chat about their feelings. Tessa was the friend who helped you bury a body and provided an alibi. "Wait, where is Damon Cove? I've never heard of it."

"It's our version of Hemlock Hollow. It's on the coast near the Florida-Georgia border," she explained.

"Cool, I love the Ocean." It's the only downside to living in Hemlock Hollow. It was a magical town near where Illinois and Missouri meet. We had lakes and rivers, but there was truly nothing like sitting in the sun on a white sand beach to heal the soul. Of course, Lucian, my wolf's mate, had a beach house out on Tybee Island. We had planned to spend a few weeks there before returning to Hemlock Hollow after the challenge. I was supposed to get to play tourist with Lucian as my personal tour guide. Neither of those things had happened thanks to the vampire transitioning thing.

"Yeah, we like it. Tell you what, if you help me find my niece Suma you will be an honorary member-."

"Wait! One of the children taken was your niece?" I couldn't believe I was being so inconsiderate to her when she was clearly hurting. She nodded her head and consequences be damned. I couldn't stop myself; I wrapped my arms around her and held on.

When she finally pulled away, I let her go and crossed my fingers she didn't slug me. Not that I would have retaliated. I wouldn't. If she needed to punch something, I'd gladly step up. Anything she needed; I was down.

"Thank you. I needed that more than I realized. Suma is my brother Thierry's daughter. She's ten-years-old and has already lost her mom to a dark witch. She's a strong little demon, but she's just a little girl, you know?" she asked.

It was clear she didn't expect an answer.

"Well, I'll do whatever I can to help find her, but unless *dad* gets his panties out of a bunch, that won't likely be much," I quipped.

"Don't let him get to you. He's overprotective of those he cares about. It's part of what makes him a good leader. Though I wish he'd get out and socialize some. All work and no play makes Lewis a grumpy boy," she teased.

"I am not now, nor have I ever been a *grumpy boy*," Lewis retorted from the doorway.

Chapter Thirteen

Lewis

After Natessa and Hector left, I got down to business planning for both our excursion as well as Hector and Lily's. I could make portals to get us where we needed to go, but we still needed places to stay and supplies. Lily and Hector could crash at my place in Fairy, and the rest of us could stay at my residence in Damon Cove. It was more than large enough for all of us. I hadn't been there to stay overnight in nearly a decade. Mr. and Mrs. Dugan managed the upkeep; in exchange, I paid them a salary as well as allowing them to live in the carriage house. They were minor demons with so little power that it was surprising they made it to adulthood. Working for me had kept them alive for the last century. They would make sure there was blood and groceries and reach out to a few contacts that might come in handy in our search. If the circumstances weren't so dire, I'd research the children's families. Searching out weaknesses and suspects would be nice. Without it, I'd need to think on my feet. Something I wasn't sure I could manage if I continued to allow so much of my focus to remain on the pale-haired temptress that was my reluctant fledgling. I thought about those locks for more hours than I cared to admit. More precisely, them splayed on my black silk sheets as I licked her pussy while she begged for my cock.

The scent of Lily drew me from the depths of my filthy mind a moment before she entered my office.

"Hector and I are ready to leave when you are," she informed me.

"I'll meet you in the garage in five minutes." I'd need that long to stand without embarrassment.

I finished my calls. Grabbed some cash and my travel bag then headed to meet the others. The garage was nearly as large as the house, but I loved cars. Old, new and all the ones between. Something about the smell of grease and gasoline just soothed my soul.

"I can't believe I'm just now seeing this place." Raine's voice had me increasing my pace.

"It is a favorite of mine," I told her as I entered the garage.

"Which one's your favorite?" she queried as she admired my 1969 Shelby mustang. The car was a white pearl with a red leather interior.

"Who could pick just one?" I replied in answer.

"True that," she chirped before the minks gave me a wink as she moved to admire the 1957 Chevrolet Corvette Base. The bright lights showcased her fair skin and hair, making her look like an angel.

I couldn't stop the smile that crossed my face at her brazen flirtation. I walked to where Lily and Hector stood next to a midnight blue Ducati. Trying to focus on the mission and not the sway of her full hips as she sashayed from one automobile to the next was harder than I wanted to admit. The bike belonged to Lily. As sweet as she looked, speed was her addiction, and the bike was only one of the three she owned.

"Are you planning to take the bike?" I asked her.

"Yeah, but also something with space, in case we need to transport the children," she responded.

"Agreed. Take the land rover. It has room to spare and will transverse most terrains," I advised.

Her bike contained a spell that allowed her to shrink it to the size of a matchbox car. If they needed speed, the bike would come in handy. I was taking two bikes with the same spells though I chose dirt bikes as they would make searching the trails that wove their way around the coastal town of Damon Cove easiest.

"As soon as you get there, check in with my father. He'll be expecting you both. Lily, do you remember where the house is from the castle?" I had taken her there many times when she was younger. As I gradually grew tired of seeking approval from a father who refused to give it, I spent less and less time there. The realm that had begun as my prison had slowly become home. I stopped seeing it as a punishment and accepted it for what it truly was: freedom. Freedom from the responsibility of a crown I'd never wanted. Vesper, on the other hand, was more than happy to step into the role.

"Yes, I remember," Lily confirmed.

"We can keep in touch with these," I told her, handing her a communication shell. They were rare and costly to gain. "I know. I don't need to remind you to be careful."

"Nor I you," she said with a smirk before kissing my cheek.

I couldn't help the smile that graced my face. Bringing Lily home had been one of the few rash decisions I'd made since my transition. A rash decision had been what led to the attack that left me as a vampire. It was a miracle my brother Vesper had walked away unscathed. A fact I thanked the heavens for.

Chapter Fourteen

Raine

Tessa and I chatted while we walked to the garage. She hadn't seen Liam or Lucian, but since Damon Cove was in the human realm, she had loaned me her spare cell so I could call them once we were there. I couldn't wait to hear their voices. Just thinking about them left a lump in my throat that was making it hard to swallow.

I must have been quiet too long because Tessa nudged me with her shoulder. "A penny for your thoughts?"

It was something Liam said often, and she knew that. She may have been closer to Luther and Esmeralda's age, but she and Liam had become close before I'd known anything about our world. There was a time when that friendship had felt threatening. Now I saw it for what it was, an attempt to cheer me up.

"I miss them so very much and I hate being sidelined. I even miss the mundane daily stuff," I admitted.

"I can't speak for Lucian since I don't know him like I do Liam, but Liam has never wavered in his love for you. Even when the rest of the world was sure you were dead, he still hoped. Witch, wolf or vampire doesn't change a thing. And if you chose Lucian, then I'm confident it won't matter to him either." Her words did little to dislodge the lump in my throat.

Too many kind words made me uncomfortable. I could feel the tears burning in my eyes, but reaching the garage saved me from the embarrassment of breaking down. Though calling it a garage was like saying the Pacific Ocean was *some* water.

I had planned to tell Tessa about my episode and how I overheard her conversation with Lewis regarding me, but the sight of thirty plus cars robbed me of thought as I took in the beauty before me. He had everything from vintage sports cars to brand new SUVs.

Hector and Lily were already there when we arrived. The pair stood next to a midnight blue bike that appeared to be made for speed. I instantly wondered if it belonged to Lewis and if so, could I convince him to teach me to ride it?

I'd always wished to learn. Roy used to talk about us buying one so we could go riding with our friends. What he really meant was I should buy him one so he could run around with his buddies and hit on anything with two sets of lips.

I darted from one vehicle to another, admiring each one's pristine condition, when I felt Lewis enter the space. I could feel his eyes on me as I admired a 1969 Shelby Mustang.

"I can't believe I'm just now seeing this place," I told him, not looking at him as I tried to ignore the weighted feel of his gaze.

"It is a favorite of mine," he told me.

"Which one's your favorite?" I asked.

"Who could pick just one?" he answered.

"True that," I chirped, suddenly feeling bold and winked at him, hoping it appeared sexy and not spastic.

His smile was sinfully sensual as he headed to where Lily and Hector stood. My pursuit of perfection, which was metal and chrome, continued. I inhaled deeply as I walked, my new senses enjoying the sting of gasoline and oil that filled the air. I liked the smell. My adoptive father had enjoyed working on cars in his spare time. The scent reminded me of the few happy memories I had from that time in my life. I used to sit and watch him work for hours.

I kept him in my line of sight, never looking directly at him as he spoke to the others. His gaze was like a magnet pulling me toward him, even when I wasn't looking. Each day that pull was getting stronger and harder to resist and watching him as he interacted with Lily was making me feel all kinds of things. I wasn't sure I should have felt where he was concerned. I much preferred the irritation I previously felt towards him over these softer feelings.

Tessa and I joined the others as Lewis handed Lily a pink shell pulsing with magic.

"We can keep in touch with these. I know I don't need to remind you to be careful," he told her.

"Nor I you," she stated with a smirk before kissing his cheek.

His smile was dazzling, yet held a touch of sadness. I moved to comfort him before catching myself.

"Are those fae communication shells?" Tessa asked, admiring the objects.

"Yes. One of the last remaining pairs," Lewis explained.

"Communication shells?" I asked.

"Think of a magical walkie talkie," Tessa enlightened.

"Sweet." I still had my nerd moments when it came to the world I now lived in.

Lily and Tessa laughed while Lewis looked at me like I had sprouted a second head.

Chapter Fifteen

Lewis

I had to turn away to hide the silly grin as Raine admired the communication shells. I kept forgetting how very young she was and how ancient I was until she said things to remind me.

Hector climbed into the land rover as Lily triggered the magic to shrink the bike before giving me one last hug and climbed into the passenger seat. I opened the garage door so they could pull out. I didn't need to be outside to create the portal, but since they needed to drive through with the land rover, it was a great deal easier to do so outdoors.

I stood in front of the Rover and pulled magic from the forest around me as well as from the air, weaving my power until a tunnel of light formed large enough for them to drive through it. They passed through to Fairy and I redirected the magic from Fairy to Damon Cove before directing Raine to the driver's seat of the Porsche Cayenne and Natessa to the cargo van that Hector had dropped off while I triggered the spells to shrink the two dirt bikes and stuffed them in my case before climbing into the passenger seat of the Porsche.

Natessa drove through first, and I directed Raine to follow. I wanted to drop off the van and head to the sight of the last abduction. If I could track them, we could be back in my realm by morning, where I could keep Raine safe. As well as keep my promise to her mates and in-laws.

We exited the portal at the end of the drive, and Mr. and Mrs. Dugan were outside before we had parked. Natessa was out of the van in a blur of movement and had her arms wrapped around the elder demon couple. Raine parked the SUV behind where she was parked.

"I guess Tessa knows them, huh?" she asked as we exited the vehicle.

"She does."

"You know I've heard of minimalists, but you act like every word costs you and you're on a Ramen noodle budget," she quipped, making me want to smile. "How is it she knows your house staff?" she seethed.

I held in my chuckle by faking a cough.

"Her brother lives here, as does her aunt, I believe. She visits often. She is popular and well-liked."

She smiled at my words, reaching for her bag as I opened the cargo area.

"I'll get your bag. Why don't you introduce yourself to the Dugan's. I think you will like them," I told her.

She nodded and clasped her hands, something I'd noticed she did when she was nervous, as she walked away. Making me wonder if she was having doubts about her self-control. She didn't know it, but she posed no danger. Vampires didn't crave the blood of demons. Their blood lacked the hemoglobin of humans and other supernaturals. Not that I feed on them, either. I didn't. I no longer drank from the source. The high could be addictive. Those vampires didn't live long. Hunters made sure of that. I had somehow been lucky enough to never catch the notice of one.

I'd make sure Raine never met that fate, either.

I watched her walk away, trying and failing, not to stare at her perfect form. Natessa's eyes met mine as Raine reached them. Her smirk said more than I cared to think about, so I turned back to the bags as if they were the most interesting things I'd ever seen.

I took several deep breaths. The gentle lap of the waves and the briny scent of the ocean had a grounding effect. Even before the attack that left me a vampire, I had spent a great deal of time here. Being a future king could be stressful. The ocean had been my haven during that time in my life. After my transition, when I was finally able to control my blood lust and think straight, I had first returned to Fairy, but when my father turned me away; I had come here. But the scent and sound of the ocean weren't strong enough to drown out the smell of blood or the beating of all the hearts I wished to devour. The demon couple were the only ones who could come near me during that time. They were the ones to suggest my realm. It cost me many favors and had started as my prison. Now it was just my home.

By the time I finished gathering the bags and reached the cottage style bungalow, I felt a great deal calmer and more centered. By the time I finished gathering the bags and reached the cottage, I felt a great deal calmer and more centered. It was nice to feel that peace again. I hadn't realized how much I missed it.

While I could hear Raine, Natessa, and Mrs. Dugan speaking in the kitchen, Mr. Dugan was busy tinkering in my office. Without considering that I had requested Raine be placed in the room next to mine out of the five bedrooms, I dropped off her bag in the adjacent room. I convinced myself it was to ensure her safety and prevent her from suffering because of distance. I told myself it was so I could keep her safe. I didn't even believe in myself.

After dropping off my bag, I headed to the kitchen to check in with the ladies before getting down to business.

"Master Damon, it has been too long since these tired old eyes have seen the likes of you around here," Rosemary Dugan told me as she cupped my cheeks, raising up on her toes to kiss me.

Something she could only manage after I bent to accommodate her because of her diminutive stature.

"Good to see you as well, Rosemary. I wish it was under better circumstances," I told her, returning her affection. I still felt odd calling her and her husband by their first names. While I was older than either of them, I was turned at thirty, but I looked young for my age even then, thanks to my fae DNA. Since they were lesser demons, they aged slower than humans. Rosemary was one hundred and four and looked to be in her sixties.

"Oh yes, of course, it is just dreadful. Those poor wee ones. I will keep them all in my prayers. I will. Frightful business,

I tell ya, I do," she gushed, hardly taking a breath, making it sound like one long sentence.

I fleetingly wondered who might get in the most words between her and my fledgling. The thought nearly made me smile, but Rosemary was spot on when she said our reason for being here was dreadful.

"On that, I must agree."

"Well, I know time is of the essence, but the body needs fuel for whatever comes next. I thought I might make a quick snack for the ladies and make you a drink while you head to your office and check in with Victor? I believe he is already in there," she suggested.

She knew I'd rushed off without thinking about feeding or what might wait for me. Something I couldn't do if I planned to keep Raine safe. If I died before her transition was complete, she would die as well. So, I agreed for her sake.

"Yes, please," I clarified, "if you don't mind bringing it to my office after the girls are fed." Raine's stomach had rumbled during the drive through the portal. I still wasn't sure what the deal was with her increased appetite, but her wolf was clearly still hanging on, as was her inner witch. I knew I needed to figure out the mystery that was Raine Hemlock, but the children needed to come first. Whatever was happening to her wasn't normal, but I didn't think it was life threatening. The situation with the missing children could be and with each passing moment, I feared it would.

Chapter sixteen

Raine

The air witch Hector climbed into the Rover as Lily triggered some type of magic to shrink the motorbike. It was clearly some type of magical charm and if we weren't on such a short timetable, I'd be bombarding them with a million and one questions, but the lives of children were on the line, so my questions would have to wait. She then placed it in her jacket pocket before she hugged Lewis and climbed in with the male witch.

Lewis opened the garage door so they could pull out. He stood in front of the Rover. I could see the magic as he pulled from the forest around his home. I watched as he weaved his power until a channel of light formed large enough for them to drive through. They passed through. Then the magic morphed and changed from vibrant green to a deep-sea blue with vivid green streaks throughout. He directed me to the driver's seat of a black Porsche Cayenne and Tessa in a cargo van. Before walking over to two dirt bikes and triggering the same type of spell that Lily had used. When the bikes were the size of a matchbox toy, he stuffed them in his bag before climbing into the passenger seat of the Porsche.

Tessa drove through first, and Lewis told me to follow. We exited the portal on a gravel lane with a large bungalow directly in front of us. The house sat on a peninsula with the ocean visible on three of its four sides.

Tessa flung the van door open as soon as she parked and darted out of the van. She sprinted to the wrap-around porch where an elderly couple stood watching us as we drove up the drive. She hugged them both and was talking up a storm to them as we pulled to a stop behind the van.

"I guess Tessa knows them, huh?" I asked Lewis as we exited the vehicle.

"She does." Was all he said.

I have no clue why, but his minimalist attitude with words really got under my skin.

"You know I've heard of minimalism, but you act like every word costs you and you're on a Ramen noodle budget," I told him sarcastically. "How is it she knows your house staff?" I demanded.

I think I almost made him laugh because he had one of those fake coughs, which made me want to smile.

I was not a fan of the swing of moods. I felt like I was getting whiplash. Living in my own skin had never felt so alien.

"Her brother lives here, as does her aunt, I believe. She visits often. When she does, she sometimes crashes here if she wants peace and at her brothers if she doesn't. She can be herself here. We all can."

I smiled at his words, reaching for my bag as Lewis opened the cargo area.

"I'll get your bag. Why don't you introduce yourself to the Dugan's. I think you will like them," he told me.

I hated meeting new people, always had. Becoming a supernatural witch queen hadn't changed that. I clasped my hands together to keep them from trembling as I walked toward the cute two-story bungalow with the wraparound porch.

Tessa noticed me before I reached the three of them. "Rosemary, Victor, this is Raine Hemlock. Raine this is Rosemary and Victor Dugan. They live here and take care of the house for Lewis. Raine is the lost Hemlock heir and a wolf... and well, I guess she's a vampire, too," Tessa explained, unsure.

"Oh, my dear, that's quite the pedigree now, isn't it?" Rosemary asked with a friendly smile. "It is a pleasure to meet you. It's about time Master Lewis found his match. He's been alone too long, if you ask me. He is always taking care of others," she gushed.

I instantly liked her, even if she was mistaken about the match part.

"Breath love," the man admonished lightly. The smile and look of pure admiration were unmistakable. "Rosemary enjoys taking care of others and the Master is so rarely here," he told me as he draped his arm around his wife. He was stout and his skin was a deep nut brown, but the carrot orange stock of unruly hair drew the eye. He had a kind smile and blue-gray eyes. He wasn't very tall, maybe five foot four, but next to his wife, he appeared tall in comparison.

Rosemary Dugan was tiny. Nearly a foot shorter than her mate. Her skin had a milky white complexion, and her silver hair had streaks of dark ebony. The dark strands gave her a chic reverse highlight effect the young humans would kill for. Her eyes were a very pale blue, and she wore a cornflower-blue smock dress with a white apron and an honest to goodness string of pearls.

I smiled at him, "Well, I hope me being here won't be too much of an inconvenience."

"Never," Rosemary assured me, leading us all into the house.

We continued to chat as we made our way to the kitchen at the back of the house. The east wall was floor to ceiling windows that overlooked the ocean. The sand was snow white, littered with driftwood. I could see a fire pit with four Adirondack chairs placed around it where the grass and sand met. The water was choppy, but I could stare at that view for hours.

Rosemary speaking to Lewis brought me back from my sightseeing.

"Master Damon, it has been too long since these tired old eyes have seen the likes of you around here," Rosemary told him as she cupped his cheeks, raising up on her toes to kiss him.

Because of the difference in their height, even on her tippy toes, he had to bend down to accommodate her. They chatted back and forth for a few moments until he headed down the hall. Rosemary got to work making burgers, and I helped while Tessa ran downstairs to get blood for Lewis. I'd noticed he drank bags of blood. They looked like the ones you'd see in human hospitals. I wondered if that was because I was with him or if he always did that. I hadn't yet had a craving for blood. Of course, at that thought, the flask Lilly had given me of Lewis's blood flashed into my mind. Just the memory made my mouth water.

"Do you like pickles?" Rosemary asked.

"Very much," I answered, still thinking of Lewis' blood.

Maybe if I tried some of the bag blood Tessa was grabbing for him, I wouldn't need him so much and I'd be able to go home sooner.

Luckily, Tessa brought a bag for me and warmed it, offering it to me as she headed down the hall in the direction Lewis had gone. I tried to down it like a shot in the hopes it wouldn't give me time to overthink it. In an effort to swallow it, I held my breath. I waited for the dark chocolate and cherries that his blood held but much to my horror it tasted just like what it was, cold thick, should never be in my mouth, nastiness. I rushed to the sink and spit the awfulness into the sink.

"Yuck! What the hell? That was gross," I blurted as Lewis entered the kitchen in a blur of movement with Tessa hot on his heels.

"What's wrong?" he asked, clearly puzzled as I stuck my mouth near the faucet, cupped my hands and frantically scooped water into my mouth and swished it around before splitting it into the sink as well.

"I think there's something wrong with the blood," I finally told him, shutting off the water and drying my face and hands.

He took the cup and smelled it before taking a small sip, then another. "It tastes fine to me," he said, offering me the cup again. "Try taking a smaller sip. Sometimes it's your human sensibilities that can make feeding from a bag difficult."

I didn't want to, but with everyone's attention on me, I tried a second time. This time making it a tiny sip, but again, as it touched my taste buds, I gagged. I made another mad dash back to the sink and rinsed my mouth once more.

"Nope, can't do it," I told him, popping the P.

"Peculiar," was all he said. Back, it seemed, to his one-word replies.

With a fresh cup in hand from the cabinet, he sliced his palm with a fingernail. He transformed into a point before my eyes and allowed a crimson stream to flow into the cup. He transformed his nail back before handing me the cup. I watched as he stepped around me and turned on the water, letting it rinse away his blood. He dried his hands, and I watched in amazement as his cut sealed before my eyes.

It reminded me of the bullet wounds that had healed before my eyes when my former friend shot and killed me.

"Try my blood. Maybe it's because the blood is cold and bagged. It's an acquired taste for some," he tells me, but something tells me that's not entirely the truth.

I wasn't sure I wanted to, but the memory of the explosion of flavor had me lifting the cup once more. Before the blood even reached my mouth, I knew it wasn't going to be a repeat. I could smell the sweet fruity scent from before that shouldn't belong to anyone's blood, let alone a strong viral male like him.

While taking small sips, I allowed the flavors to dance across my tongue. I could still taste the chocolate and cherries, but I also tasted a hint of spice and heat. I finished and handed the mug back to Lewis.

"Thank you."

If I was being honest, I wanted to drink every drop of the awesome nectar flowing through his veins. I took an involuntary step towards him before I could rein that impulse in. I sat down in the chair next to Tessa and dug into the burger. She had used some kind of spicy brown mustard that I quite enjoyed. The kosher dill pickles she had paired with them were very good. Lewis grabbed pickle and claimed the seat next to me as he munched. He studied me like he was trying to memorize my face.

I was on my fourth burger when I couldn't take his stare any longer. "What? Is there something on my face or what?" I demanded, scrubbing at my mouth.

Chapter Seventeen

Lewis

I made several phone calls before resorting to the last person I wanted to ask for help, but with children going missing in multiple places, resources were slim. I dialed the number from memory. The voicemail picked up after the third ring, and I wasn't sure if I was relieved or not. I left a message after the beep and headed to the kitchen as Natessa entered my office carrying a cup. I could tell from the smell it contained blood.

She sat it on the desk as I hung up. "Angelique, huh?" she asked.

"That obvious?"

"Nah... I just know you. There aren't many people that warrant that look from you," she informed me.

"Desperate times," I told her, downing the blood she brought me. Even after a century, I took no pleasure in drinking blood. It was merely something I required. Nothing more.

"Then we truly are at the bottom of the barrel," she stated, turning to head back to the kitchen.

I followed and entered just in time to witness Raine spitting some of the bagged blood into the sink.

"Yuck! What the hell? That was gross," she blurted, spitting multiple times before cupping her hands and slurping water into her mouth.

"What's wrong?" I asked, searching the room for an answer.

"I think there's something wrong with the blood," she declared, shutting off the water and drying her face and hands.

I picked up her cup, fearing someone had tried to target me through my blood supply. There were many who would jump at the chance to strike at me. It smelled fine, so I tasted it but found nothing wrong. "It tastes fine to me," I told her, offering her the cup. "Try taking a smaller sip. Sometimes your human sensibilities can make feeding from a bag difficult."

It was clear she didn't want to, but the girl was not a quitter. She took another small sip but gagged before swallowing and raced back to repeat the drinking from the tap trick once more.

"Nope, can't do it," she told me when she was done, making an emphasis on the letter P. It was an endearing habit of hers.

"Peculiar," I mused, thinking for a moment. She had taken my blood three times so far and had shown no aversion. I had a thought but wanted to be sure before mentioning it for fear I might get her hopes up and hope could be dangerous.

At any rate, she needed to be strong and ready for anything that might come, so I retrieved a clean cup and sliced my palm to fill the container before offering it to her.

"Try my blood. Maybe it's because the blood is cold and bagged. It's an acquired taste for some," I lied. Most vampires craved all blood, all the time, no matter its source. They just preferred it fresh from the tap, as they say.

She took a tentative sip, then a larger one, before downing the rest without taking a breath. Watching her drain my blood from the cup, the look of utter joy on her face mesmerized me. I couldn't take my eyes off of her as she handed the mug back.

"Thank you," she told me, claiming a seat at the breakfast bar.

She started eating a cheeseburger, and I stole one of her pickles as I claimed the seat next to her, admiring her full red lips as she ate, relishing each bite.

I'd been watching her through several sandwiches when she turned to me and demanded, "What? Is there something on my face or what?" she demanded, scrubbing at her mouth.

It took every ounce of willpower I had not to smile at her indignation. The woman clearly hadn't looked at herself in the mirror if she couldn't figure out why I was staring at her.

"No, of course not," Rosemary assured her, reaching across to give her hand a gentle pat. "You look lovely, dear. Not a hair out of place," she assured her.

She was right. Raine was beautiful with her pale hair and fair skin. Her eyes appeared pale with a slight pink tinge instead of red like mine. Just one more quality unique to her. If I didn't know better, I'd swear she possessed a captivating charm that irresistibly attracted me.

"If you've had your fill, we should head to town."

She nodded, climbing to her feet and taking her plate to the sink.

"Thank you so much for lunch," Raine told Mrs. Dugan, kissing her cheek on her way past.

Natessa finished the last of her sandwich and put her plate and glass in the sink with the others and hugged Rosemary before leading the way out the front door.

The drive to town was a short one. I wanted to visit the site of the last child's abduction. I would make it to each but the newest would likely be my best beat for tracking by scent, which was by far the easiest.

Chapter eighteen

Raine

The ride to Damon Cove was short, but lovely. It was a small coastal town right in the water. Tessa drove us along the waterline and down the main road, past several cute shops with multicolored awnings shading their entrances. Several had catchy names like The Black Lung smoke shop and Pet the Kitty, which appeared to be a strip club from the look of patrons waiting to enter. Though it was only eleven in the morning so I could have been mistaken. When we finally pulled to a stop, we were at the Marina. Several fishing boats and a couple of large boats that could only be labeled yachts were present, but what caught my attention was the cloud of foulness near a small play area near the shoreline.

Tessa pulled the Cayenne into the space closest to the park that held my attention as it made my skin crawl. Lewis opened my door and offered me his hand before I was ready to move closer to the darkness. Somehow, I knew that was the place we were looking for. I reluctantly took his hand and let him lead me closer to the dreadful shadow.

I was about ten feet from the small slide on the far end of the jungle gym when my feet stopped of their own accord. Lewis took two steps before noticing. Once he did, he searched my face for answers. He apparently didn't find them because he finally asked me, "What's wrong?" Looking around for threats as he did.

"I'm not sure," I told him honestly.

Tessa finally noticed we had stopped. "Everything okay?" she called, stopping as well.

She was only three feet from the slide. If I had to guess, I'd bet whatever I was seeing had something to do with the last child that went missing unless, of course, this town had more than one bad guy at work. It was always a possibility. I had learned the hard way that even in a supernatural world, people covet power. If the children or their parents were special or overly powerful, that could easily be what was happening in Damon Cove. Though that didn't explain the missing children in the Fae realm.

"I'm not sure," I repeated. This time loud enough for her to hear me. "There's some kind of shadow near the slide." I told her, pointing needlessly at the slide like she could see it. Obviously, neither she nor Lewis could see what I could. That made it likely it was some type of magic.

"What type of shadow?" Lewis asked, squinting at the area I pointed to.

"To know that I'd have to move closer, and my internal alarm system is telling me that isn't wise," I admitted.

At my words, Tessa took three large steps back and one to the side, bringing her to my left side. Lewis had stepped back as well, so he mirrored her position on my right. I created a shield and took a tentative step closer as a thought occurred to me.

I could still feel the warning bells, but they were easier to process from behind my shield. I wove an anti-magic spell into the shield, following that same hunch. The foulness was still there, but it was no longer tripping my alarm, so I continued forward until I was close enough to reach out and touch it. I wove a healing spell and a curse breaking spell, just in case it was meant to kill anyone who attempted to tamper with it, before reaching out to touch the edge of the darkness.

As I did, I was knocked off my feet and hit the ground pinned by a muscular form.

"Are you okay?" Lewis demanded, running his hands over me.

"I was until you plowed into me," I barked, climbing to my feet. "Why the hell did you do that?"

"I... thought I... saw... something..." he stammered, very unlike him.

Which had me worried I'd missed something. "Like what exactly?" I demanded, all the irritation gone from my tone.

"I guess it's my turn to admit I'm not sure," he admitted reluctantly.

"Then I guess you will just have to trust that I know what I'm doing," I told him, starting to form the shield and spells I had lost when he'd tackled me.

"I don't think that's a wise course of action," he informed me.

"Do you have a better one?"

"I might track a scent," he informed me, but I could tell he was lying.

"I call bullshit... Now what's the real reason?" I asked, crossing my arms and staring him down. Mating Lucian had taught me a great deal about winning a stare down.

"He's scared," a male voice stated, causing both Lewis and I to abandon our debate. I struck out at the strange voice, my fist aimed toward the sound, but when I struck flesh, it wasn't a stranger's face but Lewis' hand. He had blocked my fist with an open hand.

The stranger gave a braying laugh. "She's a spitfire brother. I can see why father was so intrigued. I like the fiery ones," he told me, making me want to vomit at how smarmy he was.

"Raine, this is my brother, Crown Prince Vesper... Vesper, this is Raine Hemlock. She is my fledgling and the witch queen and one of her mates is son to the Alpha of Alpha's. Please show her the respect she is due."

"Oh brother, why is it you are always so grim? You have two beautiful women in your arms and still you cannot enjoy yourself. Such a shame. Maybe I should take your ladies and show them a good time. Let them see what the fun brother has to offers," his tone said he was joking while his eyes said he wasn't.

"As one of said ladies, I think I'll pass, Prince Vesper," I told him with my widest smile and the lowest curtsy I could manage.

From the leering look I received, he missed the sarcasm.

"What are you doing here, brother?" Lewis asked. "Does father not need your help with the missing children?"

"Your ward and her friend are working on it, so I came to help you out. I thought I might be of more use here," Vesper told him.

"Is father aware of this adventure?" Lewis asked, but Vesper was already moving forward to where I could see the darkness hovering.

"So, what are we looking at here?" he asked no one in particular, ignoring his brother's question. Making me instantly dislike him.

Chapter nineteen

Lewis

My brother showing up wasn't all together surprising. Nor were his inappropriate comments. Though the look on his face when swung at him.

Raine clearly didn't care for him. Something I found I liked about her. One more of many, it seemed. Prior to my brother's unexpected arrival, Raine had been on the verge of reaching out and touching a magic that Natessa and I could not perceive. I found I didn't care for the risk to her. I'd find another witch. One that I wasn't responsible for taking care of.

Unfortunately, her lack of interest piqued his interest even more. To meet a woman that did not find him, and his power alluring, wasn't something he was very familiar with.

"Is father aware of this adventure?" I asked.

"So, what are we looking at here?" he asked, ignoring my question.

"Raine, as I mentioned, is a witch and she can see some type of darkness directly in front of where you are currently standing. We were discussing how to proceed when you arrived."

"Interesting... I can't feel anything," he stated, waving a hand through the air in front of him.

Raine sucked in a breath and stepped closer before I could stop her. She reached her hand forward as Vesper had. Unlike Vesper, the force threw her backward ten feet and into the waist-high fence marking off the play area from the water. She landed hard on the sand near the fence.

I was there in a flash, but she was out cold.

I gathered her into my arms walking towards the vehicle. Natessa rushed ahead of me and opened the rear door, but Raine's eyes fluttered as I attempted to lay her across the seat. She grabbed my arm in her strong grasp. "Whatever that was, it is very dark, and it doesn't want us interfering," she told me urgently.

"Too bad that's not going to happen," I growled, trying to climb into the rear seat with her so I could get her away from the danger.

"Agreed! Now, let me back out there so I can prove it," she barked, pushing at my chest. She was strong. There was no doubt about that, but I was ancient compared to her, as well as damn well determined...

"No," I growled, refusing to allow her to leave the automobile.

Well, until she slapped me with some type of immobilizing spell and scurried out the other door. Vesper laughed while Natessa was hot on her trail. It took me several minutes to fight through her spell and regain movement. Once I did, I was surprised to see that Raine wasn't attempting to touch the spell; instead, she was walking around the area she had previously revealed.

Chapter twenty

Raine

Although getting knocked out by whatever dark magic was involved in the abduction of these children wasn't ideal, if it taught me something about our bad guy, I'd consider it a positive even though my head was pounding and felt like it was stuffed with cotton candy...

Lewis didn't seem to see it that way. He had tried to whisk me away after one brief knock out. I should have felt worse about hitting him with an immobilization spell, but I didn't. He needed to understand I didn't like people to control me. Not even uber attractive people.

"What are you doing?" he demanded, clearly worried.

"Testing a theory at the moment," I informed him. I threw spell after spell at the shadow magic, watching to see what each one did to it as well as what my early warning system told me. When I got nowhere, I took a step closer and reformed my shield and a protection spell as I had before. I touched it for a second time.

This time, though, I threw the spell instead of wrapping it around my hand. Again, nothing happened. Finally, I pushed my shield out until I felt the surge in my defenses. Which gave me the opportunity to get a feel for how large the trigger was as well as how sensitive. I quickly found there was a weak spot in the area closest to the slide. I had to stand on the slide and allow Tessa to help stabilize me to find it. Once I did, I removed my spell and slowly inched my hand to the edge of where the shadow began. This time there was no electric jolt or being thrown into a fence, just a horrible tingling and crawling sensation which soon became a burning sensation, causing me to yank my hand back when the pain became unbearable. I jumped down from where I'd been standing, shaking out my hand and breathing through the pain. In through the nose, out through the mouth.

Lewis was there instantly, checking my injury, which was healing before my eyes thanks to my wolf genes. It had already gone from bright cherry red to pink in only moments. Super healing for the win.

It still left me feeling sad, thinking about losing these powers. I wasn't sure how I was going to deal with that loss. For the moment, I still had them at my disposal, so I intended to use them to the fullest.

"Let me see," he grumbled, grabbing my hand and examining it.

"Lewis, I'm fine. It's nearly healed now. I'm stronger than I look. I promise. You don't need to worry about me," I told him. There was no heat to my words.

He was standing so close, and the fear in his eyes did something strange to me. He was hardly touching me, yet it felt like he was touching me in all of my most intimate places. My breasts were inches from his chest and my nipples throbbed at his nearness. I had no clue how one look could leave me so hot and bothered, but when a man like Lewis Damon looks at you like he was in that moment, spontaneous combustion seemed like a valid concern.

When he still didn't release my hand, I reluctantly pulled away. Our current location and company should have been enough to quash my wanton need, strangely it wasn't. I wasn't sure how I felt about that.

Chapter Twenty-one

Lewis

I reached my crazy ass fledgling as she readied a spell to lob at the dark magic. First, a red orb followed quickly by a purple, then a blue, one after the other. Each time, the look on her face morphed. Her face was very expressive. I hardly needed words to know what she was feeling or thinking.

"What are you doing?" I demanded, worried what I couldn't see was going to harm her. How does one fight something he can't see and knows nothing about?

"Testing a theory at the moment," she informed me. She continued to lob spell after spell at the shadow magic watching it intently. Then she reached out her hand after walking in circles and even standing on the slide with Natessa's help.

Right before she jumped down from where she'd been standing, she sucked in a sharp breath, shaking out her hand while taking several panting breaths.

I was there instantly, checking her for injuries. I watched as the burn healed before my eyes. She may still have access to both her wolf and witch, but this type of healing was unheard of for a witch, a wolf, or a vampire, which served as yet another reminder of her uniqueness.

"Let me see," I told her, grabbing her hand and examining it.

"I'm fine Lewis. It's almost already healed. I'm stronger than I look. I promise. You don't need to worry about me," she insisted.

I was standing so close, and the fear was all-encompassing. I was hardly touching her, yet I was aware of her every curve. Her breasts were inches from me. They'd be so easy to reach out and caress. Her nearness was intoxicating. I wondered if she knew what she did to me. I knew I needed to step back. To get my lust under control. I just wasn't sure I was strong enough.

She was the one to pull away. Leaving me to mourn her loss.

"Well?" Natessa asked. Her words worked like a bucket of ice water to the face. It was a much-needed reality check that we weren't alone.

The *too-lovely Mrs. Hemlock was turning into exactly what I feared she might be:* a distraction. I needed to get my mind off her curves and back on the matter at hand. I did not hear her response.

"If you are done interfering, I'd like to stop wasting time. There are, after all, children missing or did you forget," I knew I was being needlessly harsh, but nothing good could come from tender feelings for her. I was only meant to get her through her transition from her becoming a monster. I was monster enough for both of us.

I didn't wait for a response; instead, I charged forward and got to work on trying to track whatever was taking the little ones. Vesper and I spent nearly two hours trying everything I could think of to track any of the children taken, with him giving unhelpful commentary.

At some point, Natessa and Raine left to grab food. Her use of her witch and wolf powers seemed to require a great deal more calories than was expected, even for a shifter.

"So, big brother, what do you say to a break? I'm feeling peckish," Vesper complained, reminding me how self-centered he could be.

Not that a stiff drink didn't sound like a great idea. It did, but the longer these children were missing, the harder it was going to be to find them.

The buzzing of the communication shell gave me hope that Hector and Lilly had had better luck than we had.

"Hello," came Lily's voice through the shell. It was a little scratchy, but clear enough to understand.

"Hello, Lily."

"Hey boss," she quipped.

"Hey, yourself. Do you have an update for me?"

"Not much of one, really. Hector can see some kind of shadow at the last abduction sight, but it doesn't seem to serve a purpose. Well, other than knocking him on his ass," Lily informed me with a chuckle.

"Yes. Ms. Hemlock had quite the same experience, yet Vesper, and I have probed and prodded without producing the same response. Did you attempt to get this shadow, or whatever it is, to respond?"

"I did. It must be a magical reaction. However, we had zero luck determining what kind. What does Miss Raine think?" Lily asked, as I knew she would.

I didn't answer for several moments, mulling over the few pieces we had gathered.

"Thank you for the update. I'll get back to you." I disconnected before she could question me further. Despite my reluctance, it appeared that we would require a witch, whether I approved or not. If I got my way, that would not be Raine. I just had to find one strong enough to keep her from getting involved.

Chapter Twenty-two

Raine

Once Lewis benched me, I stuck around for a while but when he continued to ignore *all* my observations and my gut was cramping with hunger so bad; I wanted to chew off his head to fill the void and maybe a little because he was a total freaking jerk wad. I finally asked Tessa if she knew where to get food.

Tessa took me to a place called the Tipsy Crab. It was little more than a hole in the wall, but the chowder was mouthwatering, and the drinks were strong with funny names like the pecker-head, a nasty beaver, and the passion pussy.

Four bowls of chowder and three passion pussies. Later, I had a full belly and the start of a nice buzz. The drinks were so good after number two I was even able to order them without snickering.

Tessa and I took turns picking songs on the antique jukebox as we spent hours waiting for Lewis and his brother.

"So, what's the deal with Vesper?" I finally asked Tessa three hours into our bar party.

"Normal spare heir syndrome," she informed me as we swayed to Poison's version of *Your Mama Don't Dance.*

"Spare heir?" I questioned.

"It's a royal thing. They have a second child. In case something happens to the first, the family will still have an heir to ascend the throne. Which is what happened with Lewis," she furnished.

"Why?" I asked.

"Why what?" she asked me as she stopped our strange dance, scrunching up her forehead as she tried to focus on me through the haze of liquor. The girl could hold some liquor. She had matched me drink for drink, plus several shots she did with the bartender, a big guy with a ponytail and full beard. Tattoos covered both of his arms.

"Why did he get everything that was Lewis' birthright?" I inquired.

Their father disowned him when he was changed. Father of the year, that one is not. "I know my father is old-fashioned and unforgiving at times, but their father makes mine seem perfect in comparison," she told me.

"Yeah, I met him. I'm not a fan."

"Same lady. But I think Lewis is happier not being the heir. Vesper, on the other hand, lives for all the royal bullshit," she told me as she motions for the bartender to refill our drinks.

"If he's happy, I'd hate to see him looking unhappy," I deadpanned.

Mony Mony came on and my ass shook as I danced around the bar, forgetting our conversation. I loved the song, and the buzz had me feeling frisky. A stranger with dark hair and sharp features spun me around and danced me across the small space.

By the end of the song, I was sweating and smiling from ear to ear.

"Might an old man know the name of the dancing beauty that graced our old haunt this fine night?" he asked as he kissed the back of my hand. He had a thick accent, but I couldn't place it.

He had ears that were slightly pointed, and his teeth were a touch sharper than normal, but his forest green eyes and the dimple in his chin made his features very attractive for an older gentleman. He looked to be in his sixties if I had to guess, but his smell was a combination of forest and fire, leaving me confused about his breed.

"I'm Raine... Raine Hemlock," I told him with a smile. "And you are?"

"Jacob George Thackery at your service," he replied with a snappy salute.

I liked him.

"It's very nice to meet you. And thank you for the dance. You have some moves," I told him with a smile.

"I'm honored you think so," he responded, sitting down on the bar stool next to where I'd left my drink.

He ordered a glass of red wine and another round for Tessa and me. I really should have declined, but I didn't want to hurt his feelings and it was keeping my mind off the fact Lewis had benched me.

I was still trying to work out a way to help find those kids and prove to Lewis I was capable when he walked in.

He had pulled his long hair back and braided the strands away from his face. With his dark hair like that, it highlighted his intense nose and high cheekbones, making him even more attractive.

I turned away and waited for him to join us, but he didn't. Instead, he headed to a booth in the far corner where a busty redhead had been nursing the same glass of wine for the last hour.

"Luwianos, it's been way too long, old friend," the lithe Amazonian with flame-red hair cooed with her too-perfect lips as she slid from the bench seat with the grace of a feline.

Who the hell was she and what the ever-loving hell did she just call him? I wondered, suddenly furious.

"Hello Angelique," Lewis said as she leaned in to kiss his cheek, but he side-stepped her attempt, so it ended up as an air kiss.

I suddenly wanted to yank out her gorgeous hair and claw her eyes out so she couldn't look at him anymore.

Chapter Twenty-Three

Lewis

Angelique was the last one I wanted to call, but then again, with so many children missing, the pickings were slim, and time wasn't on our side. If I didn't figure something out soon, Ms. Hemlock was going to do something stupid, and I couldn't risk that. She was my responsibility, after all.

Even after I had sent her the fire message to meet me at the Tipsy Crab, I'd stayed for another hour trying in vain to elicit a response from the shadow magic that my fledgling had found. The fact that I couldn't see it didn't help matters. It wasn't until I'd completely run out of ideas that I broke down and went to meet her.

Of course, if I'd thought that through better, I'd have known that Natessa would take Raine to the pub. They had the best food and drinks in town, and after Raine used her powers, she seemed to get very *hangry,* as the kids liked to say.

I walked in to see Raine swinging her supple hips as she danced with Jacob Thackery. The song ended and the old fire fae led her back to the bar and bought them all a drink.

I left them to it and headed to the booth where the succubus waited. Usually, I wouldn't have chosen a succubus as my partner, but since they literally transferred power from someone else into themselves, who could be better suited?

"Luwianos, it's been too long, old friend," Angelique cooed, climbing from the bench seat and stepping forward.

She leaned in to kiss me, but I stepped back at the last moment as I felt Raine's sharp gaze on me. "Hello, Angelique." I motioned to Kip behind the bar to bring Vesper, and I drinks before sitting down across from her.

Vesper grabbed our ales and dropped mine off at the table before heading back to where Natessa and Raine were.

"Not that it wasn't lovely to hear from you, but your message didn't explain what it was you thought I might help you with. Last I knew, you were against the *dark arts,* as I believe you called them." Angelique commented clearly, wanting me to apologize for some slight she felt at my label of her brand of sorcery, but it was never truer than it was now. However, my thought was if dark magic took the children, then who better to track them but another dark magic user? Not all succubae practiced dark magic. Angelique did, though, just not anything to do with children, which was why I reached out to her.

"I believe the missing children might have been taken by dark means. If that is the case, who better than a master such as yourself to track it?" I told her, purposely stroking her ego.

"Flattery is always nice, Luwianos. Yet I cannot trade flattery," she cooed, getting right to the heart of the matter.

"Isn't the safe return of those innocent children enough of a reward for the likes of you?" came Raine's angry reply before I could intervene.

She slid into the booth next to me, claiming my ale and taking a large gulp before putting it down with a grimace. "That tastes like ass. Why on earth would you drink that when they have several other much better options? My personal favorite is the Passion Pussy. Terrible name, but quite tasty." Raine ranted in the rapid manner I'd come to enjoy at some point.

"I will keep that in mind next time," I told her, doing my best to hide my amusement.

"You definitely should," she quipped with a wink. At least I think it was a wink. It was one of those quirky things she did that were all her own.

Angelique fixated her attention on Raine, and I didn't appreciate her being scrutinized, so I turned away from my fledgling and redirected my attention back to the matter at hand. "I thought if you could track the shadow we found at the last abduction site, I would grant you a single favor within limits, of course."

She was silent so long that I nearly offered more. I hated it, yet my options indeed were slim.

"I'll need a blood sacrifice and two favors," she countered.

I did not want to appear overly eager, so I fringed irritation and pretended to mull over her counter-proposal; however, her following words changed that and made my blood run cold.

"Yes, one favor from each of you should do nicely."

"Deal," Raine agreed.

"NO! NO!" I barked and tried to get up from the booth seat, but Raine had blocked me in, leaving me trapped unless I pushed her out onto the floor. "She has nothing to do with this."

"Oh, so that's how this is going to be. Well, I guess if I'm not needed, I'll just head out then," Raine started getting up from where she sat next to me and walked away.

I knew I had hurt her, but she didn't understand what owing a favor could entail in our world and I would not let her get tangled up in dark magic on my watch. If that meant she was angry with me, so be it.

Chapter Twenty-four

Raine

Joining Lewis and his dark seductress wasn't one of my wisest moves. I knew that in the back of my mind before I walked across the room. Yet it didn't stop the train wreck from happening... I blame the alcohol.

After the asshole Lewis informed the complete bar I was of no consequence, I stormed out into the briny night air. I was grateful that I didn't immediately get covered in sweat thanks to the slight breeze, despite the humidity. Anger burned through my veins as I paced the sidewalk, trying to calm my racing thoughts. I was muttering curses and pacing in front of the Tipsy Crab. I probably looked like a crazy person to anyone who drove past.

"Are you attempting to wear a path in the cement?" Vesper asked, causing me to jump.

"What the hell, dude? You shouldn't sneak up on people!" I screeched, holding my hand over my pounding heart, trying to calm it before it vibrated out of my chest. His being able to sneak up on me was a testament to how drunk I truly was.

"I did not plan to sneak up on you. I just came out to get some air. I can leave you to your cursing and pacing if you wish," he offered.

I laughed, "You're funny."

"You think so?" he asked.

"Sure, I mean dry humor isn't for everyone, but I speak fluent sarcasm so..."

"I see... So, am I to guess the expletives were for my brother?" he asked, leaning against the building and crossing his arms.

"You bet your lily-white ass they were. Got a problem with that?" I asked, crossing my arms more than ready to tell him what was what.

"Because he won't allow you to help find the children, I presume?" he inquired.

"Of course. It's stupid. I may be new to this world; however, it has been a true birth by fire, as they say, which has taught me I can handle anything I put my mind to. I don't need some controlling asshole to dictate what I can and can't do. I didn't even get hurt by that magical kick in the teeth. It hurt my pride more than anything. I know if he would just let me, I could find those kids."

"So why don't you?" he asked.

"Well... I...umm..." I stammered.

"My apologies. I thought you were some badass witch or something." He raised an eyebrow, clearly goading me.

"Actually, I'm a badass witch-wolf hybrid," I joked.

"There is no time like the present, I always say," he stated, pulling something from his inside jacket pocket.

Which nearly earned him an energy ball to the face until I saw he was holding what appeared to be a matchbox car. He sat it in the road and with a snap, an oversized neon green Humvee materialized. It was gaudy as all hell, but who was I to knock his choice of wheels? Besides, the playground where the last child went missing was a couple of miles north of the bar. Driving was much faster than walking, besides the longer I waited, the better the chances of Lewis stopping me.

Vesper was already in the driver's seat waiting for me.

I climbed in before I could change my mind.

Chapter Twenty-Five

Raine

The ride was short, and Vesper made idle conversation as he drove. He told me about Faerie. Usually, I would have found Vesper's conversation about Faerie enthralling. To be honest, I didn't hear most of it, but I did my best to nod and grunt occasionally, so I didn't hurt his feelings, since he was kind enough to help me prove a point.

He stopped the Humvee, and its headlights illuminated the playground. I couldn't see the vehicle's shadow, yet I could feel the darkness from where I sat. It appeared to be getting stronger.

Vesper got out of the car, walked around the front of the Humvee, and opened my door. I exited the car and strolled to where I knew the shadow was. I couldn't see it, yet I could feel it was still there. The smell of dark magic lingered in the warm night air. It smelled like burning leaves and rot. As I circled the area, I had a thought and wanted to test my theory, but I didn't know Vesper, and I definitely didn't want him to see me naked. He was an attractive man, nevertheless; I wasn't remotely interested. He struck me as one of those guys who would always love himself more than any other person. You know the type, those guys that are always admiring their own reflection instead of the beautiful woman he's with.

"Could I have a couple of minutes alone, please?"

I found the port-a-potties. The handicap booth was not ideal, but it was better than stripping naked in front of Vesper. I left the door unlatched, stripped my clothes off, wrapped them into a ball, and stuffed them in the changing table before snapping it closed. I took several deep breaths and cleared my mind before calling my wolf forward to start the shift.

The smell assaulted my wolf's nose, and we couldn't push our way out nearly fast enough. I'd first thought of my wolf as separate from myself, which made shifting impossible. Once the alpha helped me understand, we were intertwined. Now that I did, shifting was becoming almost second nature.

I shook out my fur and trotted to where I could now see the shadow was an opening. It appeared to be some type of rip. Possibly a crude dark magic portal, I theorized as I slunk closer, my eyes never leaving the rip.

"What the hell? Where'd you come from?" Vesper screeched backing away from me.

I just looked at him and chuffed a laugh, which sounded more like a snarl in my wolf form.

Vesper took another giant step back before asking, "Raine?"

I gave a slight nod and continued forward. I kept my eyes on the magic as I made another circuit, allowing my wolf's senses to take in what my human senses couldn't. Things such as the light emanating from within and the low hum coming from the other side. Like a siren's call pulling me forward, I stopped when my snout was mere inches from the opening. Unfortunately, there was nothing else my wolf's senses could pick up. I pulled on my witch powers; the power came, but it was sluggish. I growled my frustration as I made one more circuit around the opening. I was nearly positive it was a portal of some kind and that the sound lured victims to their death. But they were expecting children. I was much more than that. The question was whether I could overpower who or what was on the other side.

The truth of the matter was not in my current state. I couldn't. Due to my fatigue and slight buzz, I couldn't. My shift had made that manageable. With that thought in mind, I made one more pass around the opening before heading back to the port-a-potty and shifting back. Once I did, I hurried to dress while forming a plan to return once I was at full power and I knew just the potion to hurry that process along. I just needed to phone a friend to get the ingredients I needed.

I hurried back to the Humvee, making Vesper jump when I climbed into the passenger seat. He was sitting in the driver's seat, scrolling through his phone.

"Damn it, woman, you scared the hell out of me. Well, don't keep me waiting. What did you learn? Anything helpful?" He asked.

For some reason, I still wasn't sure if I could trust him, so I lied, "No, nothing. I guess Lewis was right to discount me," I told him with a shrug. The words tasted rancid on my tongue, but I said them anyway. "Can you drive me back to Lewis' house? I'm suddenly exhausted." That last part wasn't even a lie.

We drove in silence back to the house. I jumped out and headed inside with a small wave, and a thank you.

Chapter Twenty-six

Lewis

Angelique and I bartered back and forth for a while, her still wanting Raine as part of the bargain, and me continuing to decline. The more we talked, the more I knew I had done the right thing getting her to leave.

Thankfully, Vesper had gone out to check on her. Nothing would happen to her while in the company of the future King of Faerie.

Natessa waved as she too left a short time after Raine had stomped out. I hated to admit it, but she even made that look sexy as hell. Unfortunately, the longer we were together, the harder it was becoming to remember why we'd never work. Why I couldn't get attached, because when she learned who I truly was, she'd never look at me as anything but a monster and she'd be correct. I needed to remember that because she was a woman who could easily break me.

By the time Angelique and I had agreed, Kip was getting ready to close for the night. She left to get her supplies. I was meeting her at the playground at three in the morning. Something about the witching hour. I didn't understand, but I wasn't a succubus.

I paid my tab as well as Natessa and Raine's, and left Kip a hefty tip. It was my small way to help the people of Damon Cove since we weren't the traditional pack. We were a group of *unusual people that* had banded together, more tribe than pack.

"Have a good night, sir," Kip told me as I opened the door to leave.

I had a random thought and turned around. "Kip, have you noticed anyone new around town? Is there anything suspicious?"

He appeared to be thinking as he wiped down the bar. "We have had a few strangers pass through on their way to other places. Nothing out of the ordinary, though."

"Human or sup?"

"One human, the rest sups. Though now that you mention it, Eva has had her future witch-in-laws here for a visit. Don't know much about them except they are from Hemlock Hollow," Kip informed me.

"So, are they witches? Do you know?"

"Yeah, they're witches. Eva brought them the other night for our seafood boil. Have to say that Paul scored big time with that mate of his. Too bad I'm not a witch," he joked.

I might have had a thought or two along those lines as well. Not that I would admit as much out loud.

I planned to called Eva in the morning. It wasn't likely the witches were involved, but I needed to be sure. I thought taking Raine might make it easier. Her being their Witch Queen and all.

Chapter Twenty-Seven

Raine

Once I got inside, I raided the kitchen. I ate some kind of roast, potatoes, and some homemade mac and cheese. Some of Lewis' blood would have been nice, but my powers no longer felt sluggish when I called them, so it would have to do. I ran to the room Lewis had dropped my things in grabbed my cell phone from the bag, and dialed Liam. It rang three times and went to voicemail. I didn't leave a message. I dialed Lucian's cell next, which again went to voicemail. This time I left a brief message telling him where we were and asking him to call whenever he got my message. Once again, I attempted to reach out to Liam and left the same message as I had left for Lucian. It shouldn't have surprised me it was midnight in Georgia, meaning it was one in the morning in Hemlock Hollow. I could have called Hemlock House, but if they were asleep, I didn't want to wake them and knew Reggie most definitely wouldn't have the same consideration. He carried his duties a bit far when it came to me. Heck, maybe all the talking felines did, but I'd only met the one thus far.

I tried Becca next, but again, there wasn't an answer, so I opted to skip the spell until morning.

I threw on a pair of black leggings and an oversized gray tee with a pair of flip-flops in the fanny pack. A trick I stole from Lucian's sister Payton. She hated cars, so she often ran in wolf form from one place to another so she would stuff her things in a fanny pack so she could carry them and not be stuck naked when she shifted back. Once I was done, I slipped out onto the balcony and jumped the twelve or so feet to the ground. I stripped out of my jeans and cute blue blouse, stuffed them under one of the deck chair cushions, transformed and slid my snout into the strap of the fanny pack, and took off. I may not have what I needed for a spell, but a better look at the portal was definitely in order.

I hightailed it back to the playground so I could figure out what was on the other side of that portal before Lewis realized what I was up to. It took me less than 20 minutes to get there. Once I arrived, I searched the area around the shadow before I stepped out into the open. The closer I got to the opening, the more apparent it was that the portal was closing. The opening was nearly half the size it had been just an hour prior. That decided for me. If I didn't act now, I would likely miss my shot, and if my jailer found out I was here, he'd never leave me alone again.

Going alone wasn't ideal, however, as dark as the magic used to create it was, my internal alarm bells weren't ringing.

With the alcohol no longer clouding my senses, I could smell clove, overly sweet and musty. It left a foul taste on my tongue, and I had to suppress a gag. I could still hear the ethereal music and feel the pull, except it wasn't nearly as strong as before, supporting my thought that it was closing.

I wondered what that meant. Did they have all the children they needed or were they just picking another place to open a new lure? Or did one have nothing to do with the other?

Slowly creeping forward, I listened intently for any change in the song. I briefly worried that it might close before I was through and rip me in half. I could see my pale silver fur covered in guts and gore—half of me in Damon Cove and half of me who freaking knew where. With that cheery ass thought in mind, I backed up five paces and prepared to sprint through in hopes of my ass and all making it through in one piece.

As my face reached the opening at full speed, something struck me in the side hard. I rolled ass over tits through the portal.

Chapter Twenty-eight

Lewis

It was already after midnight when I left the pub. I rode from the oldest abduction site to the most recent. I even drove past Eva's and looked for any unfamiliar cars. If Eva's family really was here and were witches, it wasn't likely they drove, but there was an SUV with dark windows and Georgia plates. If Eva's family was from Hemlock Hollow and did indeed drive, their plates should be from Illinois. It was always possible it was a rental.

By the time I reached the last and most recent I was beginning to feel fatigued. I didn't require a great deal of sleep, but my body did need to rest. My muscles could fatigue, however, not nearly as quickly as they would if I was still fully fae. With under two hours before I was to meet Angelique, I decided the play area parking lot was as good a place as any to wait and nap. I parked the motorbike then laid down on a park bench and admired the night sky. One of my favorite things about Damon Cove was that it was small, and everyone knew everything about their neighbors. Hopefully, that would make finding the person who took the missing children easier. If Angelique couldn't help, I knew I would have to eat crow and ask Raine. I had no doubt that given enough time, she could do anything she put her mind to. The problem was if by some terrible stroke of fate, the person behind all this was a local, they were most definitely going to regret it when I found them, and I did not want Raine to ever see that side of me.

I shook the thought from my mind as my eyes slowly drifted shut. I enjoyed listening to the sound of the ocean waves lapping at the shore. It soothed me. As a child I used to lay near the waterfalls for hours in Farie. That sound was the one thing missing in my personal realm. I was just starting to mull over how to add it when I heard something.

I sat up and looked around. The silver wolf was prowling around where Raine had said the shadow was. The same place where the last missing child was seen. It didn't take long for me to realize who the wolf had to be and that she was about to do something supremely stupid, which is exactly what she did. I watched as she crept slowly forward and then stopped. She backed away several paces, and I knew what she was planning. I sprinted forward in an attempt to stop her. I reached her and wrapped my arms around her wolf middle as we fell through a portal, unlike anything I'd ever seen.

We tumbled through darkness for only a few moments before we landed hard. Our momentum flipped us several yards into a forest, tangled around each other. The ground was littered with sticks and stumps. My arms were ripped from her when I slammed to a jarring stop as I collided with one of said stumps. It hurt like hell but the scream of pain from Raine was worse. If she was screaming that meant she had shifted, and she didn't strike me as the type to transform, leaving herself naked in an unknown situation if she didn't have to. Her scream was one of pain leading me to believe she was hurt and hurt badly. With her vampire healing, it could only mean one thing. I was up and moving before my eyes could register what I was seeing. Blood and way too much bare skin were all I registered. She was no longer wailing. I couldn't decide if that was a good thing.

The sound of unknowns approaching had me at her side in half a heartbeat. She was impaled on an ancient fence post that had rusted barbed wire wrapped around her torso. She was unconscious and it looked like the post broke when she hit it and the wire was the only thing holding her up. She was suspended several inches off the ground. Her own weight caused the barbs every few inches along the wire to embed further into her pale skin.

I could hear the voices moving closer, making it necessary to free her. I knew it was going to hurt her. There was no way around it. Without the luxury of time, all I could do was free her and hope her healing kicked in while I dealt with our guests.

I ripped the part of the fence post off that was sticking out of her left shoulder. It had luckily missed the bone, but the muscle, tendons, and ligaments would smart for a bit, but the damage should knit closed as soon as the wood was out before I did that I needed to remove as much of the wire as I could.

That would be easier and faster without her moving and with unknowns approaching fast was the name of the game. I moved as quickly and gently as possible the entire time listening to their progress.

Chapter Twenty-nine

Raine

My assailant's momentum added to mine and propelled us through to the unknown. We landed in a wooded area. I didn't get to see much with Lewis wrapped around me as we tumbled the first few feet after passing through the opening, but he was snatched away from me as I tumbled several feet further as branches and stumps pulled and tore at my body. I struck something hard, slamming to an abrupt halt. White-hot pain lanced through my whole body. The pain was so severe I lost consciousness but not before the searing pain forced me to shift back to my human form, leaving me naked and bleeding in an unknown forest. Yep, definitely not my wisest move.

I have no clue how long I was out, but it wasn't nearly long enough. One moment I was floating in darkness, the next my eyes flew open as agonizing pain yanked me from oblivion.

I tried to scream as the pain racked my body, but a large hand was covering my mouth. My fear nearly wrenched me back under until Lewis' lips at my ear gave me something to focus on other than the pain and fear.

"We have company coming," he hissed, his tone husky. His hot breath sent shivers down my spine.

He removed his hand from my mouth which is when it finally registered that I was naked, and he had me cradled against him. My back to his front and his proximity coupled with my nudity did things to my body that were most definitely not appropriate. My core clenched and my nipples hardened. I should have been embarrassed about my body's response to his touch, but I wasn't. Focusing on the muscled male form holding me helped distract me from the burning pain in my shoulder and chest.

He moved away and offered me his shirt. The view of his well-defined muscles was interrupted by the sound of dogs barking and pounding feet moving our way at a rapid pace. That was the bucket of ice to the girly bits I needed to cool my racing libido. I pulled his shirt on trying not to enjoy the smell. My ears told me we had several visitors about to join us as well as multiple canines. The scents also told me they were human, not supernatural.

I'd learned the hard way that human weapons were a threat to supernaturals just as they were to a human. It just took more bullets to get the job done. For me, it had taken three.

Not that I didn't understand their fear. I did. Any being that ever wished to survive knew to fear something stronger and more intelligent than them. Supernaturals lived longer, had magic, protected their own, and had a dozen other characteristics that made them superior to humans. It was a basic truth, pure and simple yet two single supernaturals would be hard-pressed to deal with multiple assailants. Especially if said assailants had weapons.

Lewis pulled us behind a boulder, and I watched as he wrapped vines around us as our visitors broke through the tree line less than thirty feet from where we hid. It didn't take long before the dogs caught our scent, but when one tried to poke his nose through to where we hid, I growled low enough that the humans wouldn't hear it while Lewis created a breeze to push our scents along creating a false trail leading them away.

"Nice trick," I told him when they were far enough away, I didn't think they might hear us.

"You too. It takes me a few moments to switch between elements," Lewis explained.

"That makes me want to ask a ton of questions, but I think we should get out of here and look around before they come back," I offered.

He parted the vines he had wrapped us in and climbed out before offering me his hand. Since my shoulder was still hurting and my range of motion was still slightly limited, it was much appreciated.

"Do you know where we came through?" I asked him since I had no clue.

"About five hundred feet that way," he told me pointing off to the left.

He directed me past the fence and back into the trees near where the humans had been. As I'd feared, there was no sign of the portal. If that was due to it being visible only from the other side or because it was now closed, I couldn't be sure.

"Anything?" Lewis asked.

"Unfortunately, no."

"Then why would the humans be walking around out here in the middle of the woods at such an early hour?" he mused.

"And why did they have guns?" I wondered.

"How do you know that?" He asked.

"Do we really have time for stupid questions?" I seethed before answering, "Because I could smell them."

"Possibly because they are afraid of something other than us," he mused, opening a portal back to the park.

"Wait, aren't we going to look around? Follow them? Something?" I demanded.

"It's dark. We don't know where we are or if they are even the bad guys we're looking for," he replied as he stepped through the portal he'd created and waited for me to follow.

I wanted to argue, but he wasn't wrong, nor was he entirely right.

"Give me something personal to you," I demanded, holding out my hand.

He removed an onyx ring and handed it to me. I ran back to where we had hidden placed the ring in the grass and ran back to where Lewis stood waiting on the other side of the portal.

"Did you just take my ring and throw it in the grass?" Lewis asked though he seemed more intrigued than angry which made me smile.

"Yep, sure I did. You said it yourself: We don't know where we are, but if I leave your ring here once we are back in Damon Cove, I can track it back to here. That way, we can figure out where we are and come prepared for whatever awaits us," I explained as I stepped through to the park.

Chapter Thirty

Lewis

When Raine took my ring and dropped it in the grass, I was sure she had lost her mind or that she wanted to piss me off. Once she told me her plan though I knew Natessa was right when she told me I should let Raine help. As much as her sneaking out had pissed me off, if her trick worked, I'd forgive her transgression.

When we returned to Damon Cove, Angelique was waiting. As much as I didn't want her help, I knew she would hold me to our deal, so I decided to let her attempt her dark magic at one of the other sights since Raine already verified that the current one was closed. We were fairly confident she could get us back to where it let out.

Raine noticed her as well, "I'll leave you guys to it and see you at home... I mean your house..." she said, backing away from me.

"Raine-," I started, but she shifted to her wolf form shredding my shirt as she did and took off down the beach.

Angelique's dark laugh drew my attention from her silver fur as she fled.

"Enough," I barked, already irritated with her.

"It's not my fault your new pet can't handle a little competition," she purred.

"You are not now, nor will you ever be her competition! Understood?" I growled.

"Touchy much?" she cooed. When I said nothing, she continued, "Where did your *friend* say this shadow was?"

"There's been a change of plans. This one has closed so I'd like you to attempt your spell or whatever at one of the other sites," I informed her, turning and walking away without staying for her reply.

Angelique had worn shoes with heels better suited for solid ground, so I reached the bike and had to wait for several minutes as she fought her way across the sandy ground.

"You could have offered me some assistance," she whined.

"You can follow me," I told her, ignoring her comment.

Once she was in her car, I started the bike and headed to the following abduction site. Unfortunately, she wasn't able to help in the least. It was a huge waste of time and spending time with her when all I wanted to do was check on Raine, had my nerves on edge.

"This isn't getting us anywhere. It was a long shot, but it's late, so let's call it a night."

Again, I didn't wait for her response before turning to leave.

"A deal is a deal, Luwianos," Angelique yelled as I roared away leaving that as a problem for another time.

The ride was too short. Usually I would have rode until I had shed the worry and doubt that had become my constant companion since bringing the vixen that was my charge into my life.

Natessa was sitting on the porch with a glass of juice when I returned.

"Well, I hear the two of you are getting along swimmingly," she deadpanned.

"I am not in the mood," I told her sitting down next to her.

"Any luck?" she asked, all business.

"Not with Angelique no. But Raine might have, even though she defied me to get it and nearly exposed herself to a bunch of armed humans."

"I *heard* the reason she was *exposed* is because *someone* tackled her rolling them both through a dark portal ending with her impaled and naked and she still thought of a way to figure out how to get back there," she stated clearly siding with her friend.

"So that's how this is going to go, huh?" I asked, feigning hurt.

"Yep. Boobs before balls," she replied.

"Who the hell thought that was an apt motto?"

When she merely laughed, I knew it was the pissed-off vixen I could hear snoring upstairs.

"Of course," I chuckled. "Did she get a hold of her mates?" I asked, hoping something good could come of the day.

"She did. They quite enjoyed her stories about you," she teased.

"I'm sure they did," I laughed easily hearing her as she regaled them with her tales of how terrible I had been to her. It wasn't without reason, but she didn't know that.

Chapter Thirty-one

Raine

I ran aimlessly for a few miles as I seethed at the thought that Lewis thought the fiery-haired siren was better suited to helping him than I was. Killing her was always an option, but I didn't think me ripping her apart would endear him to me. No. It'd only prove he was right to keep me isolated from the people I loved for fear I might lose control.

So, I ran until my gut was twisting with hunger, and I no longer wanted to feel Angelique's blood on my lips. Only then did I find my way back to the cottage for a stiff drink and several heaping plates of food? I vaguely worried Mrs. Dugan might be upset with me, but my body needed calories, and the woman could cook. Everything was flavorful. I ate until Tessa came down to join me. Then I told her about the night she missed. By the time I was through we were both laughing so hard we were crying. It helped immensely.

When Liam and Lucian returned my call, I tried my best to stay awake and tell them everything they'd missed along with the hell Lewis had put me through. Lucian seemed more on board with my plan to find the children and then skip town for a much-needed mate moon. Whether that would require death or maiming was open for debate. Lucian was sure it would. Liam just gave me his, *your being the stubborn voice*. I both loved and hated that voice. Mainly because it was the one he used when he felt I was in denial or being overly difficult. He seemed wired to know me better than I even knew myself. Making him my sweet mate, while Lucian, on the other hand, was more blood thirsty, making him my, *help bury the body* mate.

I fell asleep while still listening to their voices as the sun began to rise.

I WOKE UP SEVERAL HOURS later, drooling on the phone that Tessa had loaned me. Unfortunately, it was dead as a doornail, dashing my hopes of calling my mates to say good morning. So, I took a quick shower and went in search of a charger for the phone.

I followed my nose to the kitchen, where I found not only bacon, eggs, and hash browns with homemade sourdough toast but also Lewis sitting at the table, which shocked me. The clock in the hall had told me it was afternoon, and I didn't expect to see him there.

Clearly, Angelique hadn't been up to the task, or he wouldn't have been sitting there, right?

I schooled my face to hide my glee at that idea and ignored him as I took the farthest seat away from him. Mrs. Dugan placed a large cup of coffee and a plate heaped with food in front of me. I thanked her and dug in.

Lewis was reading a real newspaper and didn't appear to notice my arrival. I wasn't aware those were even still a thing, nor did I buy he had missed my arrival but decided two could play his game. I was nearly done eating and had stood to refill my coffee when he broke.

"You'll want to put your refill in a to go cup," he said, not looking away from his paper.

"Why's that?"

"Because he's taking you to Hemlock Hollow to get the supplies you need for your tracking spell," Tessa told me, handing me a to-go mug as she winked.

She knew that Reggie had brought me the supplies I needed last night. He was part Brownie, which allowed him to travel from one point to another in the blink of an eye.

"I'm ready," I chirped, trying to hold in my delight at seeing Liam and Lucian.

"The sooner we track our way back to where the dark portal spits out, the better," Lewis added, dashing my excitement.

Lewis made a portal to Hemlock House, and as soon as my home came into view, I couldn't control myself, I ran like hell. Through the opening, across the lawn, and into Lucian's waiting arms. He stepped out the front door only a stride in front of Liam who was beaming as Lucian passed me to him once he was done kissing me thoroughly. Liam did the same before placing me back on my feet between them. They each wrapped their arms around my waist as we watched Tessa and Lewis approach. I pulled them each as close as humanly possible. I just needed to feel them near me. The pain I'd been feeling faded to nothing, as I relaxed into their hold.

Chapter Thirty-two

Lewis

When Natessa initially suggested I take Raine home to gather supplies for her tracking spell I refused. But after she pointed out that it was the fastest way to get both the supplies she needed as well as allow Raine to see her mates who she was missing a great deal. She reasoned that allowing her to see them while we could only stay a short time would both incentivize her and allow me to gag her control with the strong emotions sure to be present at seeing them after all this time.

I wanted to decline, but her logic was sound. Plus, her energy was off since returning from the shadow portal. I hoped seeing them would tell me why.

As soon as I told her, I knew the glee in her radiant smile made it worth anything that might follow. I opened a portal to her home, and she squealed as she ran through the opening as soon as it was large enough for her to pass through. Natessa had called them so they would be there to see her. Of course, if I'd thought that through all the way I might have realized that seeing her in their arms would be difficult. More so than it should have since I'd spent so little time with her, and most of that was while she was unconscious. I wasn't sure what was wrong with me, but it was clear having a fledgling was as bad an idea as I thought it was going to be and as soon as she was safe to return to her mates, I'd return to my life and forget she existed.

"Let's get this over with!" I told Natessa tersely.

"Chill Uncle Grumpy. Give her a few minutes. She's earned it," she told me, leaving me standing there alone.

I followed her through a few moments later returning my feelings to the dark box where they belonged. They were all standing on the porch waiting as I walked through.

"Thanks for letting our girl stop by," Lucian said with a smile. He had his mother's storm blue eyes and his father's dark blonde hair.

"Yes, thanks so much. You don't know how much we have missed her," Liam, her other mate, added.

I gave them a nod in response.

"Well, come in and tell us what you are planning. Reggie is gathering some fresh wolfsbane. He said you wanted something fresh to boost your spell?" Liam asked as he led us inside his arm still wrapped around Raine as she beamed at him.

It took almost an hour for the talking cat, A.K.A Sir Reginald III, Reggie for short, thank goodness, because calling a cat, talking or otherwise, Sir wasn't something I felt comfortable doing without laughing, to gather the fresh supplies Raine would need. During this I sipped chi tea and watched as Raine told her mates and Natessa tales of her time with me. When she told them about my father's visit, I nearly joined them in their merriment.

She had a way about herself that drew people in. Even Angelique was intrigued by my young fledgling, which I did not care for.

It wasn't until we were waiting for Raine to say her goodbyes that I realized her power was no longer humming in my ears. All morning, even while she slept her powers had buzzed in my ears like a nest of angry hornets. Now I heard nothing. I had no clue what caused it, but I felt that being near her mates had fixed whatever was causing it. She was practically blinding me as she shone with light and power as she exited the house. So much power.

She skipped across the yard wearing a smile so wide I don't know which was brighter, her power or her smile. I was still pondering that as she enveloped me in a firm hug.

"Thank you, thank you, thank you... This means so much to me. You don't even know how very much I appreciate this. I know you didn't want to have a fledgling, and I'm sure you never expected to end up shackled to the likes of me, but I promise-"

"Raine...Raine," I finally interrupted. "You are welcome. However, we truly should get going on that tracking spell. We don't know how far we will have to go or how long it might take."

"Of course," Raine agreed, waving one last time at both her mates who still stood on the wide porch. She had a beautiful home, and unlike when I visited most places, I didn't feel like I was wearing a pair of pants that were a couple sizes too small. Nut huggers were not on my list of things I ever wanted to do, but I imagined that's how it might feel.

In her home, I only felt intrigued.

Chapter Thirty-Three

Raine

I know it was wrong to go along with the lie that Tessa told so I could see my mates, but once I walked through that portal, okay, I may have *run* to my sinfully sexy mates like an ape with my ass on fire, but I'd do it a thousand times over to feel their arms wrapped around me. I loved them so very much. It shouldn't be possible to love two men who were as different as night and day, but I did. Liam, with his kind blue eyes and dark hair was my boy next door. He has loved me for the whole of his life. Even before he knew me, I'd only had the honor for a few short months. Lucian was my dark broody wolf that only showed his softer side to select people. I was proud to be one of the rare few. Together we were going to be a family, and I couldn't wait.

I'd been so full of energy and excitement by the time my short visit was over that I'd hugged Lewis. Initially he was stiff, but he relaxed into it by the end. We were still far from friends, but I wanted him to know how much I appreciated the short visit even if I didn't always act like I did.

After releasing Lewis, I turned one last time to wave at my mates and blew them both kisses before turning around to follow Tessa through the portal back to Damon Cove. I was hoping that the dark portal had only taken us a short distance.

Once we were back in Damon Cove, I didn't waste time assembling the spell. I chose the side yard at Lewis' house, and once I was done assembling the tracking spell, I waited until Tessa joined us before igniting it. As soon as I did, a golden magic ribbon unfurled to the east. We had agreed to take the van in case we got lucky and found the kids and the two motorbikes in their shrunken form in case we didn't and needed to make a quick getaway.

Following the spell was slow going and draining, but after almost two hours, we had to abandon the van when we reached the forest's edge. It took another twenty minutes on foot before we found Lewis' ring. Like the night before, there was nothing in the immediate area, so after arguing for several minutes, of course, Lewis reverted back to thinking I was incapable of protecting myself again.

It only took one small zap with my power to remind him I wasn't without weapons. We each picked a direction and walked. Every fifteen minutes, we checked in by cell phone. At minute twelve of our third check, I reached a parking lot with five motorcycles in front. At first glance, there appeared to be an open garage door, and rock music was bellowing out. From where I stood, I couldn't tell if it was a shop, but I had three minutes before needing to check in, so I walked around the area, staying within the tree line, keeping out of sight of anyone who might be watching from inside. There were lawn chairs and tables made from the wooden rolls used for bulk wire near a fire pit and cornhole game. A second garage door at the back of the building formed a drive-through when both were open.

Through the door at the back of the building, I could see a large, bearded man sitting with a cap over his face and his feet propped on the seat of a motorcycle that looked to be missing a motor. Several other bikes missing different parts were scattered throughout the area. A couple of beat-up couches lined one wall, where two other men also lounged. It appeared to be a motorcycle club of some sort.

I wasn't close enough to determine if they were supernatural or human, but there was no sign of the dark magic that had formed the portal. The timer went off, signaling it was time to check in with Lewis and Tessa. Once we were all on the phone, I told them what I found, but Tessa had found something worth reporting. She dropped a map pin so we could find her.

Halfway to where Tessa was waiting, my internal warning niggled, putting me on alert. I slowed my pace but kept moving while staying alert. The closer I got to my destination, the more I was sure Tessa had indeed found something. What? That was the question.

Chapter Thirty-four

Lewis

The mere suggestion of splitting up had me feeling like I had a gut full of battery acid, but it was two against one, and since I had no plans of ever hurting either of the headstrong women if I could avoid it and unfortunately, they both knew as much. So, when the saucy minx zapped me with her power, I caved and agreed to a compromise, trying my best not to smile at her antics.

We communicated while each walking in a different direction. I found nothing but trees, weeds, grass, and tons of nothing, as did the ladies until the third call. Then, both of them found something. Natessa's sounded the most promising, so she shared her location and Raine and I headed her way.

We'd need to check on the motorcycle garage as well but not until after.

I was nearly there when I heard Raine to my right. I changed my course and intercepted her.

"Can you feel it?" Raine asked by way of greeting.

"Feel what?"

"It's like the dark portal but a thousand times worse," she told me as I slowed to match her pace. Normally she moves so fast that she's hard to keep up with but the closer we got the slower she went. "The closer we get, the more uncomfortable it gets," she finally informed me.

I would have told her she could stop, but I was learning that she did as she liked, and telling her what to do only made her dig in further.

By the time we reached Natessa, I still couldn't *feel* anything but could hear something. A high-pitched whine was emitting and getting louder the nearer we reached where Natessa stood.

Natessa had indeed found something; the question was, what?

Like me, Natessa could hear the high-pitched whine. However, she could also see darkness, which I could not. Raine could both see and hear the thing. Putting all of that together, it was clearly another portal of the dark variety.

From what Raine was able to see, it sounded like this might be the one that led us to the children. All we could do was hope we found them alive. So, as much as I would have liked to plan, get supplies, and research what we had found, I knew we couldn't risk not following through now while we could.

Or that had been the plan. Instead, we were able to push our way past the repelling spells only to hit a brick wall. None of us could see it yet; that's what it felt like. It was down to each of us being able to trace every brick.

We each gave it all we had, but to no avail. We couldn't break through, which begged the question of whether or not it was too late to help any of them. None of us said it, but it was clear that was the worry on all our minds.

Once we had tried all we could without more resources Raine set a magical snare and we walked back to the van where we portaled back to Damon Cove for food and brainstorming. Since we still needed to check out the biker area Raine had found, we grabbed takeout and went back to the house for blood and to touch base with Lilly and Hector. They hadn't reported in yet, so I wanted to at least talk to my father and let him know we might be making headway. Since he had reached out for my help and then sent Vesper as well, I wanted to attempt to keep the peace.

Chapter Thirty-Five

Raine

Tessa had indeed found something darker than dark. It felt like the shadow portal Lewis and I had tumbled through on crack. It was like standing near a downed powerline. It made my teeth feel like they were vibrating. It was an altogether unpleasant feeling.

We had each given the oily darkness everything we had, but we couldn't break through. I was sure whoever or whatever had taken the children was on the other side, but without a great deal more power, we weren't getting through. Our best hope was to catch someone coming or going and make them take us through, but we didn't have time to wait around.

I left a magical trap that wouldn't stop anyone from coming or going, but it would alert me when they did. Then, I would be able to get past their magical security. I was sure of it.

Lewis took us back to Damon Cove. Once we had provisions, we returned to the house so Lewis could check in with Lily and Hector. We were all hoping they had found something more promising. If not, we would need to gather more power and kick our way through.

The Tipsy Crab's special of the day was lobster scampi, so we grabbed enough for an army.

Tessa and I were grabbing plates and whatnot, so we could eat when my internal warning flared. I turned, searching for the source when the most delicious scent I'd ever smelled assaulted my senses, my gums ached, and my mouth watered. I turned to find Lewis had sliced his wrist and was filling a cup. My attention was glued to the blood as it dripped into the mug.

Once the cup was full, he reached for the faucet. In a flash of motion, I darted forward licking his wrist before I could think better of it as soon as my lips clamped down my eye teeth elongated. I looked up into his eyes as he watched me. His gaze caused heat to blossom in my core eliciting a moan from my lips as I licked and nibbled his skin.

"Looks like I'm just in time for the fun." Vesper's words were like a bucket of ice water to my overheated pussy.

I yanked away, the heat now in my cheeks. Lewis handed me the cup of blood, but I couldn't meet his eyes as I realized I still had elongated canines and I wasn't sure how to make them recede.

"It will be easier once your hunger is sated," Lewis offered.

Of course, it would. I didn't want to drink Lewis' blood with everyone's eyes on me, but I could feel the truth of his words. I needed the smell of his blood washed from the air before I was going to be able to get my fangs to obey my command.

I gulped it down in three large swigs not meeting their eyes and smothering the moan that wanted to crawl from my throat at how delicious it was. It still weirded me out that I needed blood even if Lewis' tasted better than anything I'd ever drank.

Tessa saved me by handing me a heaping plate of lobster scampi and I sat down at the table. The blood had sated my appetite but the scampi like the chowder was a pleasure to the taste buds.

I took my time eating as I listened to Lewis fill his brother in on everything we'd found since they last spoke. Then he excused himself to reach out to Lily and Hector for an update and to check in with his father.

As soon as Lewis stood Vesper started bombarding me with questions about my mates.

"So, you have two mates?" he asked.

"Yes."

"Both are okay with sharing? I heard one was a wolf. I have yet to meet one that wouldn't take a man's head for looking at his mate let alone f-" Tessa cut off what I was sure would have been something sleazy.

"Why the interest Vesper? Thinking of applying?" Tessa asked.

At this point I excused myself but not before hearing what she said next.

"You might want to get to know her before you try to become her knight in shining armor, she's a force of nature and can be downright scary if you piss her off," she told him laughing.

Chapter Thirty-six

Lewis

"You might want to get to know her before you try to become her knight in shining armor, she's a force of nature and can be downright scary if you piss her off." I heard Natessa tell Vesper as I came up the hall.

He smiled and gave her a lecherous wink, reminding me of the Vesper from before he was heir. The one I did my best to avoid back then.

"Oh, I see you're still that guy—the one who's itching to get his teeth kicked in. I guess you do then. But please make sure I'm there to watch, I'd love to see it or actually, I'll record it so I can replay it," Natessa told him laughing.

Vesper stomped off as Raine joined us.

"Lilly and Hector have anything to report?" she asked, clearly ignoring my brother's attitude.

"No... I didn't get an answer."

"Is that normal with communication shells?" Raine asked.

"It is decidedly not. They are magic, there should be no reason for one of them not to answer me at all times," I explained.

"Is there another way to reach them?" she demanded.

"There is not. Which means we need to find something to get through that doorway we found and then go find them."

What I hadn't told her was that they had not only not answered but also missed a check-in. I didn't want to add to the problems we already had, but neither Lily nor Hector would ignore my calls.

We were planning to portal to Hemlock for more supplies before portalling to the opening but when Raine's snare called all that went out the window. Instead, we headed to the opening praying it'd still be open or that there'd be someone we could make lead us through.

Raine and Natessa ran to grab what supplies they could from the small batch of spells Mrs. Dugan kept on hand as well as from a local witch. There wouldn't be anything offensive, but I made sure there were always defensive spells made by witches I trusted as well as transport charms. None had near the strength that Raine did, but every little bit helped in a crisis.

Once they joined us outside, I opened a gateway that let out fifty yards into the tree line near the portal Natessa found. The first thing I noticed was the absence of the whine we'd heard the last time.

"Raine, do you hear anything?" I whispered, stopping everyone with a hand gesture.

"No but the slimy evil is still here," she confirmed. "And whatever set off my snare is still there. I can feel them."

We advanced slowly, ready for whatever we might find.

A baylar demon stood guard next to a garage-sized dark portal. I did not have the senses that Raine had yet even I could feel the darkness emanating from the thing now that it was open.

"What's our play?" Natessa asked.

Vesper took the response out of my hands when he fell over a log and cursed, drawing the demon's attention. Baylar demons are short, stout, slimy green creatures with scales and a forked tongue. They walk on their back legs and spit acid that could melt inch-thick metal.

The foul thing skittered our way making a loud hissing sound as it readied to spit.

Vesper froze it and the portal started to shrink at a rapid pace.

The next thing I knew my damn fledgling's ass was diving through the opening. Natessa looked from me to the closing portal before smiling and following behind her.

Chapter Thirty-seven

Raine

Lewis opened our step-through a little ways from where we'd found the closed door of darkness. We stepped through and I could immediately feel the dark energy I'd come to recognize as the portals used to take the children.

Lewis heard the hissing before I did. However, when we reached the portal, we found a squat, slimy green creature with scales, a long snout, and a forked tongue, reminding me of an alligator crossed with a troll.

The foul thing skittered our way, making a loud hissing sound before we attempted to advance. Vesper shot a bolt of icy magic, and two things happened at the same time: the magic froze it in place as a perfectly macabre ice sculpture, and the opening began to quickly shrink.

Knowing time was short I didn't think, I merely acted. I dashed forward through the rapidly closing opening before it could close, cutting off our only lead. So, I ran like my ass was on fire and hoped it worked out for the best.

I was spit out into a snowbank. The sky was dark, and the smell of malicious magic drifted in the air. As I looked around at the frozen ground with its light dusting of snow and the barren trees, I briefly wondered if my first trip to another country was going to be via a cursed portal while hunting for abducted children. Tessa tumbled through a moment later knocking the thought from my head as she knocked me on my ass. Both Lewis and Vesper followed her through the nearly closed opening. We all searched for threats as we took in the area where we'd been spat out. It was clear we were most definitely not in Kansas anymore.

"What the hell," Lewis whispered as he crouched beside me.

If I hadn't known better, I'd have thought he was worried about me.

"I figured we needed to seize the opportunity to save those kids while we had it."

"Agreed girlfriend," Tessa told me before looking at Lewis, "Now that we're here what's the plan boss?" Her cocky smile told me she agreed with my decision and if I hadn't jumped through, she likely would have.

"We need to split into teams of two," Vesper answered before Lewis could, "Raine and I will go this way while you and Tessa go that way," he continued.

"No!" Lewis barked, "We stay together. We don't know where we are or what we will encounter."

Normally, I would have objected, but my Spidey sense, if you will, told me it was a bad idea to leave Lewis' side. Something told me he was going to need me. I knew it was irrational, but I'd learned the hard way to follow my feelings.

It wasn't long before we picked up the sound of people in the distance. Well, Lewis and I could; Vesper and Tessa didn't have super-sonic hearing like we did. We advanced slower after that. Once Tessa and Vesper could hear them, Lewis stopped us again with a hand signal.

"I can hear something that might be the children. Now we split up. I can't pinpoint their exact location, but I can tell there are several people," Lewis told us in a hushed voice.

They headed right, and we went left. Our plan was to skirt the property's border, meet on the other side, and compare notes to decide our next steps.

Chapter Thirty-Eight

Raine

As we skirted the border of the property, staying in the trees, it was clear that several people were there. However, from where we were, there wasn't a chance in hell of smelling their species. We were only a quarter of the way around and had already counted at least ten sentries standing guard. It was clear the place was more than the simple farm it appeared to be.

The sound of a crying child pulled my gaze to the tent erected in the farmhouse's backyard. It was made of heavy green canvas, reminding me of large army tents.

"That is most definitely a child. Do you think they are all in there?" I asked in a hushed whisper.

"I don't know, and we can't risk going in until we're sure where they all are. We can't risk them being harmed. That means none of your Lone Ranger business," he told me quietly but smiled, softening his words.

"Understood."

When he looked at me and raised an eyebrow, I added, "Cross my heart," using my index finger to do just that. Then, I gave him a cheeky smile and a wink.

Lewis shook his head as he picked his way across the snow. I had just spotted movement in the tall grass ahead when he grunted. I spun, but he was gone. I slowed my pace as I smelled the scent of his blood. Turning to follow the divine smell, I spotted his shoe in a puddle of blood. Some of it was Lewis's, but the majority wasn't, which made me immensely happy. Thankfully I couldn't examine that feeling due to the sound of crunching boots on the snow. I wasn't sure how, but I knew it wasn't Lewis. I ducked behind a tree as a figure moved toward me. From his scent, I could tell he was a shifter and bleeding. The smell of the blood made it hard to tell anything more than that, so I waited.

As he reached me someone else walked our way, "Daniel, get your ass over there and relieve Buck. Maybe then he'll stop his fucking bitching. I swear I'm done with this gig. The money isn't worth the risk," the newcomer complained.

"Yes, sir," the other replied, turning back the way he'd come.

I waited as he moved closer. He texted and stopped next to a tree only six feet away. I was worried I'd been discovered until I heard the unmistakable sound of trousers unzipping.

His smell said he was human and armed with a gun. Since I couldn't see him holding it, it was obviously a hand gun.

While I had promised Lewis I wouldn't do anything stupid, I had no clue where he was, and the man was a human and had his dick in one hand. So really, there was very little risk. Right?

I pulled power to my hand and stepped forward, slowly inching toward him, crossing everything I had that he wouldn't turn around before I reached him. I couldn't risk tossing a spell and missing. I may be vampire fast, but that still didn't allow me to outrun a bullet. I had learning to be good at many things since joining the supernatural world, throwing things and hitting a target aren't in that list.

I reached him as he was zipping up, one touch to the back of his neck had him going night, night and none too soon either because someone was moving in the trees in front and to the left, of where I crouched.

Using my magic, I pulled shadows to hide my form. I waited until the figure stepped from darkness into the moonlight. Vesper crept forward, searching the area. He had a gash to his forehead and was holding his arm at an odd angle. I didn't see Tessa anywhere. I dropped the shadows and stood when he was close enough so we could speak without raising our voices. There was a creepy ground fog that made everything appear more sinister.

"Vesper."

"What the hell, woman!" he hissed, stumbling back.

I gave a low chuckle despite our situation.

"Sorry. Where's Tessa?" I asked, keeping a watch for signs of the enemy.

"I'm not sure. We were attacked," he said, indicating his head and arm. "Where's my brother?"

Something in his tone had my hackles up, but since I'd lost Lewis as well, I couldn't really say much.

"I don't know. He was next to me one minute and gone the next. I do know he was injured, but I can't tell you if it was life-threatening. I was looking for him when you showed up."

"I'm sure he's okay. We need to find those children and get them to safety before they are drained and discarded," he stated.

While I knew what he said was the truth, something told me Lewis was in more danger than the kids were in that moment.

Chapter Thirty-Nine

Raine

"I know that is the logical conclusion, but I have to find Lewis first," I stepped to the side to go around him without waiting for a response.

He grabbed my arm. The hair on the back of my neck stood on end, and I growled, only just stopping myself from zapping him with enough electricity to power a small town. Thankfully, I reminded myself he was only thinking of the children and was smart enough to remove his hand quickly. At this point, I continued on my way.

I didn't turn, but I heard him follow me a moment later. I wasn't thrilled to have Vesper as my partner, but since I'd found him it made sense to stick together.

"Did you and Tessa find anything before you got separated?" I asked, following the smell of Lewis' blood.

"We thought so, but it wasn't anything. Then we were attacked, I fought off my attackers, but when it was over, she was gone. I tried to find her, and I found you instead," he explained.

I nodded as I realized I was no longer following Lewis' blood but his actual scent, which meant he had healed, as Vesper had predicted. Yet somehow, I didn't feel reassured.

I stopped as we reached the back of an old barn. There was no cover for a good twenty feet around it. We watched as two men stepped out a small door and lit cigarettes. This effectively blocked me from knowing if Lewis was inside and if they were human or supernatural. With Vesper still guarding his left arm, I would be facing both on my own blind. I knew I wasn't a weakling, but despite how being around Lewis made it appear, I liked to think I was cautious by nature.

"Let's check the far side and see if there's a safer way in. If we get lucky, we might be able to rule the barn out," I suggested.

"And if the children are in there and my brother isn't, then what?" he demanded.

"Then, as long as they are safe, that's where we will leave them."

"And what if they appear safe and they are stripped of their power while we are out here stumbling around in the cold searching for an immortal vampire?" he asked, clearly not used to people who didn't do things the way he wanted them to.

"Fine, if the kids are in the barn, you can wait with them while I find Lewis. Then we will come back and rescue them unless you want to port them to Damon Cove. Then we'll meet you there."

"And what if something happens while I'm twiddling my thumbs? I only have one damn arm in case you haven't noticed," he said again, indicating his arm.

"Oh really? Huh, I guess that escaped me. You are a future king; act like it!" I barked, before adding, "Besides, if the children are in there and Lewis isn't I won't be far just yell, and I'll be here to rescue you, malady," I mocked, adding a bow just to piss him off.

The conversation had been moot because as we rounded the barn and the cigarette smoke cleared from my nose, it was clear both our targets were inside leaving only Tessa missing in action.

"Good news, both the children and your brother are inside. The bad news is that Tessa isn't, but we can deal with that after the children are portaled safely back to Damon Cove. However, first, those two guys smoking over their smell like they are human, still at least one of them has a gun, which with you hurt isn't an idea," I told him, trying to think all of our options through.

"Even with only one arm, I can handle two humans," Vesper replied.

"You heard the part about the gun, right?"

He shot a blast of ice at the ground before responding, "I got it."

"Fine. I need to get close enough first to find out if Lewis is a prisoner or if he's working on getting the little ones out. Keep a watch out while I do."

Chapter Forty

Lewis

I have no excuse for the bear shifter catching me unaware except that my focus was on making sure my too-sexy fledgling, with a heart of gold, didn't get any ideas in her head about going rogue. By the time I killed him, I'd drawn enough attention that a couple of humans managed to put a few bullets in me. Since they were using silencers no one would likely know. I took one to my right arm and another to my left thigh.

While it usually wouldn't have been a major deal, the bullets were iron, and I was still fifty percent fae. Getting them out took some time, and the blood loss had left me weaker than a human, which is how I ended up shackled to a support beam in some type of barn.

My head felt full of dandelion fluff and my muscles felt like over cooked noodles. I did my best to shake it off and take in my surroundings. There were at least four assailants with guns, and my shackles were, unfortunately, iron, which was not ideal, but if I knew my fledgling, she was already tracking me. Hopefully after she met up with Natessa and Vesper because at least four or five of the children were also being held there. With the one we heard in the tent, almost half of them were still unaccounted for. I prayed to the gods that had long abandoned me that we did not find them too late.

I tried not to think about what that might mean for them while I looked for a way to free myself.

A chain rattling behind me drew my attention in time to see a stock of fuzzy orange hair, duck back behind a stack of straw bales.

"Hey, it's okay. I won't hurt you," I told her in my most reassuring tone.

I wasn't good with kids. I'd never been around them unless you counted Lily, but she was more adult at ten than most adults, so I never had.

I had nearly given up on the tyke returning when a bright blue eye peaked around the straw again. I smiled, attempting to see how close she would get. It looked like it might be a little girl, but she was so dirty I couldn't be sure. The shirt looked like it might have once been pink. Judging by her size, I guessed her age to be six or seven.

"Hello, I'm Lewis. What's your name?" I asked, glancing behind me to see another kid. This one was a boy older, closer to preteen age. He was thin and tall with almond skin and dark hair. He wore an antimagic collar, however, unlike the little one he didn't appear to be chained.

"Her name is Ruby. She's a fire demon. That's why she is chained with all the explosive stuff around her. She burnt two of those thugs and the building they were keeping her in, even with her antimagic cuffs. She's pretty badass for a seven-year-old girl," he declared proudly.

The idea that their captors had chained a fire demon with all the flammable products around her insuring she would likely kill both herself and the other children, was cruel. Adult fire demons could withstand direct fire for an extended period of time. A child her size could not. I could not wait to make them pay for every moment they had held the children before ending their miserable existence.

"She sounds very brave. How about you? What's your name?"

"Markus," he replied.

"Nice to meet you, Markus. My friends and I have been looking for all of you. We're here to take you home. But with these on," I lifted my hands, indicating the cuffs, "I can't do much. You think you can find me something to break these chains with? Then we can get all of you out of here and back home."

The boy shook his head, yes, before disappearing quietly. I kept an ear out for our captors while I waited for him to return. It was several long minutes before Ruby poked her head around the bales of straw.

"Hello, Ruby."

"Are you really here to save us?" Another voice asked from somewhere above me.

I looked up to see a tawny pair of eyes peeking through the spaces of the loft floor. The eyes said shifter, yet the scent said witch, telling me she was likely a hybrid like Raine. Which was, of course, no surprise, as most of the citizens in Damon Cove were. Until a few months ago, it was one of the few places where they could be safe and be themselves. A slip of a girl was changing all that, and I was man enough to know when this was all over and she returned to her town and her mates, I would miss her. Being around her kept things interesting, whether one liked it or not. I found I did.

"I did indeed," I told her.

"Walter, too?" the voice asked.

"Of course. We came to take you all home. Your parents are all distraught."

"And what if I don't have any?" a boy with umber skin and pointed ears marking him as fae asked.

I didn't want to lie to him, but I also wasn't sure how to answer that question. The creak of a rusty hinge saved me from having to. I put my finger to my lips to indicate he should be quiet. Once, he nodded and melted back into the shadows with a solemn nod. I dropped my head forward, closing my eyes, pretending I was still knocked out. In the hopes one of my captors might get close enough, I could take them by surprise. Even with the iron I still had my vampire strength. I had to hope it was enough.

When I was captured, my attackers were mostly humans and shifters. Shifters were strong and fast, and the majority had claws or talons that hurt like hell, but I could take a great deal of damage before going down. The only reason they managed to take me was that they had a dark witch with them.

Chapter Forty-one

Raine

Ituned into all of my senses as I crept to the edge of the tall grass. Once I was as sure as I could be that it was clear, I darted to the door and slipped quietly into the barn. It smelled of hay but the musty scent of age which accompanied it, as well as the lack of any animal sounds or recent smell of them, said the place wasn't in use. At least not for animals, at any rate.

Among the normal musty barn smells, there were many old scents, both human and supernatural. There weren't initially any sounds of movement as I crept down a central opening with stalls on both sides. I'd passed several of them before I heard movement above my head, followed by straw and dust. I readied a stun spell, looking up. It took several minutes before finally seeing a huge brown eye staring through the planks of the loft. The small fingers wiggling above me caused me to smile despite the circumstances. I put my finger to my lips in the universal symbol to be quiet and the eyes bobbed, so I continued forward.

I was halfway down the row when a reed thin preteen with dark hair appeared at the end and motioned me to follow. I increased my pace until I reached the end. Then I slowed and poked my head around the corner, where I found Lewis chained to a support beam. A small red-haired child sat a few feet away from him, giggling at something he was doing. The boy stood halfway between Lewis and me. I was headed his way when I heard the creak of the door that I had entered a few minutes before. As I was heading his way, the creak of the door, which I had entered a few minutes before, caught my attention. I darted the rest of the way and crouched next to him.

"Are you okay?" I whispered, examining the cuffs and shackles holding him.

"I'm fine. Just hurry and get the kids out," he told me.

Of course, the man objected to being saved by a woman. I seethed as I knelt next to him, his essence flowing over me, and the heavenly scent of his blood had my heart pounding and my hands sweating. I'd like to say it was because of adrenaline, but the warmth between my thighs told a different tale.

"Just shut up and tell me how to get you free?" I barked, ignoring him as I examined his restraints.

"Why must you always be so stubborn?" he demanded.

"Because I no longer do things just because others think I should."

The distinctive sound of a gun cocking had me spinning around to find three men. My nose told me they were human and also that they had more weapons than the gun that one man held. I could smell the gunpowder and metal and old blood. Which smelled sour, and old, not like Lewis', which was a sweet nectar. Again, my mind was drifting when we needed to focus. I shook my head to clear my thoughts. His blood was muddling my thoughts, so I took several steps away from him to clear my head and get my bearings.

While we were arguing, the bad guys had gotten the drop on us... Again.

I pulled the magic to one hand while transforming the other, readying my claws for whatever came my way. I was treated to a huge helping of disappointment when Vesper swept in to save the day. He threw ice blades, dropping each of them from behind. Not my style, but whatever worked, I guess.

"Hello, brother," Vesper joked, "Noticing that you seem a little tied up."

I ignored him as I used my magic to get the cuffs off.

"Shut up, Vesper, and make yourself useful. Go release the kid that's chained behind those bales. Go slow and take Markus. Ruby trusts him," Lewis told his brother.

"Who the hell is Markus and why me? I don't even like kids," Vesper continued to mutter as he walked away.

I smiled as I had a fleeting thought of what it might have been like to have a sibling. I quickly quashed the thought. There was no reason to wonder about things that never were.

Chapter Forty-two

Lewis

Raine melted the iron cuffs while Markus gathered the other children. Ruby had hidden when Vesper went near her, even with Markus' encouragement. She refused to come out, so Raine stayed with the three children while I tried to convince her. I still didn't know why on earth she would listen to me, but I tried because it meant she would be okay.

"Ruby, it's okay. We are going to get all of you out of here, but first you have to come out," I pleaded, trying to keep my voice low. We needed to get a move on before someone came looking for the three guys my brother had taken out. There had been a great deal more than those three on my way in to contend with and with the kids. We were sitting ducks.

"You promised you'd help Walter," Ruby whispered from between the straws.

"I will Ruby, but first you need to come out and we'll get everyone home," I reassured the girl.

"Home?" she asked, finally crawling out.

I waited for her to come to me. "I need to get those chains off you first, though. Then you can show me where Walter is so we can get him, too."

Once she was next to me, I crouched down slowly and took her chains in my hands and snapped them with a quick tug. The cuffs on her wrists and ankles had enough room to get a finger between her and the metal and snap them. The collar was a different story. I couldn't break it without risking hurting her. Removing it was risky since we didn't know if it could be tracked, but using brute strength wasn't going to accomplish it, and I didn't want to risk the kid getting burnt. If Raine used magic to melt them, or if she even could. The girl had been chained with normal chain, unlike the iron, me and Markus had been wearing.

Once that was done, I offered her my hand and led her to where Raine and Vesper were standing with Markus, a green-skinned girl with pink hair and small horns protruding from her forehead and an ebony skinned girl.

"There's still another boy, but we haven't been able to find him," Raine explained.

"That must be Walter," I told her. "Do any of you know where he might hide?" I asked the kids.

"He's probably near the tent." Markus explained that someone had taken his sister, Willamina. "They're twins and since they sucked all his magic out, no one really keeps track of him. He doesn't even have to wear one of these," he told us, showing the anti magic cuffs he and the others wore.

That wasn't something I was prepared to hear. It was bad enough to worry that the children might have died, but hearing that one had been stripped of their magic was heart wrenching.

Raine and I saw the tent while we were scouting. Raine had wanted to go in, guns blazing, but I made her wait. I needed more information than she did to get things done. She followed her gut. I couldn't be that trusting of my inner beast. He was bloodthirsty and savage. I had to keep that part of myself caged.

I shook the thoughts from my head. I could not change my past, nor could I go back in time to save the girl. All I could do was move forward and pray for the best. Before the fledgling landed in the middle of my life, I hadn't relied on anything but my strength and prowess. Since she came along, I'd spent more time asking for help from a higher power than I had in all my demon life.

"Okay, so here's what we are going to do. First, we need to portal the kids back to Damon Cove, then Vesper and I are going to come back to get Walter, Willamina, and Tessa. Then we will get everyone home," I explained.

Raine looked like she was ready to argue, so I added, "Raine is my friend, and she is super powerful. No one will hurt any of you while you're with her. Now everyone join hands and she will lead you through. Once you are all through, I'll close the portal and you will all eat some of Mrs. Dugan's famous chocolate chip cookies while we get the others."

With that, I open a portal to home.

Chapter Forty-Three

Raine

I didn't like the idea of Lewis going or technically staying while I took the kids back to Damon Cove, but I was trying to trust he had a plan that wouldn't get him killed. So, I took the smallest girl's hand and once we were all forming a chain, Lewis opened a portal to his front yard.

Mrs. Dugan was out the door and sweeping the children into the house before Markus, who was bringing up the rear, was even through, as her husband held the door beaming at his wife.

I turned to tell Lewis to hurry his ass up when the sound of gunfire had me sprinting back through as it rapidly closed.

Lewis' back was to me and, with bullets flying from multiple directions, I didn't want to distract him. I didn't see

Vesper as I dove behind a piece of old farm equipment, taking some of the attention off the hard-headed vampire.

I tossed an energy ball at one gunman and ripped the throat out of another one with my teeth. His blood tasted awful like lake water, slime and sulfur. He must be some type of water shifter. What kind? I didn't have a clue. I spit as much of it as I could out. It was at this point that Lewis noticed my presence. To say he wasn't pleased would be an understatement.

He snapped the necks of two men while I took out one more with a kick to his knee. Once he was on the ground, a roundhouse to the noggin was all she wrote. The floor was littered with bodies and the silence rang in my ears after all the chaos and noise.

"What are you doing?" Lewis demanded.

"Looks like I'm saving your ass, pops!"

Vesper appeared out of nowhere, looking around at all the bodies littering the barn floor.

"I leave you for five minutes and this happens," Vesper added. To me he said, "Thought you were staying with the kiddos."

"Both of you cut it out and get your damn heads in the game," Lewis told us in a clipped tone.

While I felt duly chastised, his brother smiled like we were just out for a casual stroll. He strutted through the bloody mind field with his dark hair and his form fitting suit, like he was walking through Sak instead of a barn filled with corpses.

Lewis followed him and I brought up the rear. My internal alarm still wasn't going off, but something about the situation wasn't adding up. I just had no clue why I felt that way, but since I started following my gut, it hadn't led me astray.

With that in mind, I increased my pace and positioned myself between the brothers. Lewis gave me an odd look. However, for once, he said nothing. We marched down the worn path toward the tent, near the back of the dilapidated house. There wasn't a single soul in sight, nor were there any normal animal or insect noises.

I scoured my memories, trying to remember if that had been the case when we'd been trudging through the snow looking for the kids. I knew when shifters were around that it could affect the behavior of animals, yet I couldn't recall anything about insect activity being affected.

The back of the tent didn't have an opening, but the boy from earlier shimmied under the bottom edge.

I put my finger to my lips, showing he should be quiet, but he darted back the way he came.

"Well shit," I muttered. "I'll follow him while the two of you enter through the front."

Lewis looked like he might object, but Vesper pulled him along behind him.

"Five minutes and we go in. You get the children, and we'll take care of anyone else," he told me, still pulling his brother behind him.

Chapter Forty-four

Lewis

Vesper had no sooner stepped out of my line of sight when all hell broke loose. Men descended on me as I held the men at bay long enough for the last of the children to pass through the portal. Once Markus stepped out of the barn, I let the portal close as I spun to face the onslaught of assailants headed my way.

Luckily Raine had gone with the kids, so at least I didn't have to worry about keeping her safe for the first time in more days than I cared to count. I shook the vixen from my thoughts as I focused on the bullets flying around me. Since I'd already gotten shot with iron bullets once that day, I wanted to avoid a second-round if at all possible.

I snapped out, connecting with the first one's chin in a spine crushing hit as I moved to the next, dropping one after the other. A scuffle behind me drew my attention. I swiveled, ripping another's head from his shoulders.

Raine had dropped one attacker and was making short work of number two. Which left only her and me standing.

"What are you doing?"

"Looks like I'm saving your ass, pops!" she sassed.

Vesper returned, looking around at all the bodies littering the barn floor.

"I leave you for five minutes and this happens," Vesper added. To Raine, he said, "Thought you were staying with the kiddos."

Raine flipped him off while he lunged in her direction.

"Both of you cut it out and get your damn heads in the game," I told them in a clipped tone. Heading for the door without waiting to see if they followed.

Vesper followed with Raine, bringing up the rear. The night was eerily silent as we made our way to the large army style tent we'd seen earlier while scouting the area. I worried Natessa was still missing, and I'd still not heard anything from Lilly and Hector.

Halfway there Raine and Vesper traded places, but the scent of dark magic hung heavy in the air which was keeping my nerves on edge. Aside from the attackers in the barn, there had not been a soul in sight, living or dead.

We moved at a brisk pace, reaching the back of the tent in under five minutes.

The boy from earlier, Walter, crawled under the back of the tent.

Raine put her finger to her lips, but he crawled back inside the tent without responding.

"Well shit," she muttered. "I'll follow him while the two of you enter through the front," she told us, laying on her belly and crawling after him.

I wanted to object, but Vesper pulled me along behind him toward the front of the tent.

"Five minutes and we go in. You get the children, and we'll take care of anyone else," Vesper told her as he towed me in his wake.

I looked back as we rounded the corner, but she was gone already.

Chapter Forty-five

Lewis

I moaned as I rolled onto my side and icy pain shot through my left shoulder.

"Motherfucker," I muttered, panting through the pain.

I lay there in the dark, fighting off waves of nausea as my head pounded out a heavy metal ballad, using my brain as their stage. I attempted to ignore the pain so I could get my bearings.

I was lying in a dark room. The floor was rough, possibly concrete or rock of some type. The air was cold, stale, and dank. I listened for movement in the dark. The scuff of a shoe, the whisper of clothing over skin, anything to tell me where I was and who had captured me.

It wasn't like I was a young one. I'd trained in all manner of combat and weapons. Despite having both vampire and fae powers, I had been surprised twice in a very short period.

I pushed through the pain and ignored the self-recrimination while I took stock. I found myself shackled with iron again, which wasn't ideal. I hadn't yet fed, and they sapped my strength and blocked my fae power.

The shackles limited my range of motion, but having some movement was better than nothing. My left shoulder, where the bulk of the pain originated from, had a wound which was bleeding freely. That likely meant I hadn't been out long, otherwise my vampire healing would have taken care of it.

I spent the next several minutes checking my pockets for anything to help me get the cuffs off so I could get back to Raine and Vesper. I could only hope whoever had gotten me hadn't gotten them as well.

The exploration turned up nothing. Whoever searched me was thorough. I worked myself into a sitting position. It hurt like the devil and took longer than it should have. I had to stop twice to let the stars retreat from my vision before I could continue.

Once I was finally sitting, I looked around the dank space. Thanks to my vampire sight, I was able to make out the cell I was in. There were no windows and a steel door with no window or handle that I could make out. My vampire hearing wasn't picking up a thing. If I had to guess, it was some type of magical charm. Likely courtesy of their dark witch. Yet another reason to kill her when I next saw her.

WARRIOR

I had no clue how long I was in there before someone opened that door. When they finally did, I couldn't believe my eyes.

Chapter Forty-six

Raine

I crawled under the bottom of the tent in search of the boy. What I found shocked the hell out of me. The tent was empty but for the boy and a girl strapped to a chair in the center of the empty space.

I strolled forward, looking for hidden threats.

"They're gone," Walter told me, his voice loud in the empty night.

"Where'd they go?" I asked, continuing to scan for hidden assailants.

His only answer was to shrug.

"I'm Raine. My friends and I are here to help," I told them as I reached them.

The boy stood next to his sister, whose gaze followed my every movement. They'd fastened her to a metal folding chair with her hands behind her back. Instead of anti-magic cuffs like the other children had worn. They secured her with iron, and it burned her where it touched her skin.

"I'm Walter. This is my sister, Willamina. Can you get the iron off her?" he asked me as I walked around the chair.

Vesper's ice magic had kept me from burning the other children when taking off their cuffs and those hadn't been iron. I circled the girl a second time before a plan formed.

"I can, but it might not be very comfortable," I admitted, or pretty, I thought, but didn't say it out loud.

They had secured her arms to each bar, forming the back of the chair and each ankle to the front legs. She was yet to respond, so I asked, "Is it alright if I try to get you loose?"

She looked at me for several long moments. Taking my measure. She finally nodded.

I sent Walter to find something heavy to use to break the iron once I was ready. While he looked, I worked out what I would need to do. Vesper had used his ice power to allow me to melt the anti magic bands the other children had been wearing. Someone had made the anti-magic bands the other children had been wearing out of a softer metal. Since these were iron, the metal was a harder quality metal, which would hopefully benefit me.

Walter found a thick metal pipe that was a couple of feet long that would work perfectly for what I had in mind.

"Alright Willamina, I'm going to get these things off of you so we can all get out of here."

Her large blue eyes welled with tears as her bottom lip trembled faintly, but she set her jaw and shook her head *yes*.

I took a slow breath and flexed my trembling hand, attempting to release the fear and worries that were attempting to overwhelm me. Fear of what might have happened to Lewis, of failing to save the rest of the kids, of something happening to Tessa, of never seeing my mates again, and so many other things that I didn't have time to think about.

After taking one final deep breath, I focused on extracting moisture from the atmosphere. Liam was into nature spells. He'd been teaching me a few. Pulling water from the air around us was one of them. I wasn't as good as him, but since he wasn't there, I would make it work. Normally I'd close my eyes, but since I wasn't sure where everyone had gone or when they might return, that would have been stupid.

I concentrated as I cupped my left hand, forming a cup. I spent several minutes waiting and while I could feel the water; it wasn't working.

"Maybe if you use your other hand to focus on the water. Like to direct it. That's how our nana says you should do it," Walter offered.

He might have been young, however. He was fae and their magic was based in nature, so he probably knew better than I did.

"What do you mean?" I asked.

He showed by using his index finger to form small circles above his hand.

I repeated the motion. He nodded, so I attempted again.

A gasp had my eyes flying open. I hadn't realized I'd closed them until I heard the sound. A funnel of water hovered in the air over my palm. The sound had come from the boy. I smiled at him and directed the water to drizzle into my cupped palm. I directed the water over the cuff, securing the girl's left ankle. The angle was awkward, and it took two tries, but I accomplished getting the metal coated with a few tablespoons of water.

Freezing it once it was there was trickier. I yanked the bottom of my shirt up and tore it, using my teeth to get it started. When I had a good strip, I poked it into the space between the girl's skin and the iron. Then I created a spell to drop the temperature, keeping it small and localized. I touched the metal around her ankle. I repeated the process with each one. After they were all frozen, I picked up the pipe.

"Now comes the tricky part. If there's still anyone close, they will hear this and come for us. That means two things: first, I have to be quick and second, we all need to be ready to run like hell once the last one is off. Deal?"

The twins both nodded.

I took another fortifying breath and everything that I did not miss and maim the poor girl. Briefly, I morbidly wondered whether or not my healing potion could heal it if I did.

I shook off the negative thoughts and got into a position to strike the first cuff. The first iron cuff took three strikes before it broke. After all the cuffs were off, I pulled the one and only transport charm I had thought to bring from my pocket.

I had planned to strong arm Lewis after we saved the kids to allow me to go back to Hemlock Hollow to spend some quality time with my mates. Now that seemed selfish, and all I wanted was to get these kids back to safety. So, I could figure out what happened to Lewis, Vesper, and Tessa. My list of missing friends was ever growing and becoming worrisome.

Chapter Forty-seven

Raine

I turned to the twins. "Once I drop this, we will need to hold hands and walk through the smoke together." They were already holding hands, so Walter took my hand.

At least, that was the plan. Truth was, I didn't know for sure where we were, and transport charms had limitations. I hoped that with my added power boost, it would be enough. If not, I could end up with us all gods knew where.

I dropped the charm and envisioned Lewis' front porch, then we stepped into the smoke. I could smell the Georgia marsh grass and magnolias as we exited in front of Lewis' house.

Mrs. Dugan was out the door in a blur, her gray hair frizzy and cheeks flushed. She pulled the twins to her ample bosom.

"Come inside. Their loved ones have already picked the others up, but there is plenty left to eat, and then I will work on getting the two of you home," she told them as she led them inside. "Miss Tessa is in the master's office. You should grab some food and join her. I'm sure there's much to talk about."

I did as she suggested and grabbed several sandwiches, as well as a soda. As I was leaving the kitchen, Mrs. Dugan handed me a small thermos. Even with the lid on, I could smell it was Lewis' blood. The scent of dark chocolate and ripe cherries made my mouth water.

"Thank you," I told her, and she clasped my wrist to keep me from walking away.

"I don't know what is going on, but I know it can't be good if he doesn't return with you. He told me if you returned without him to give you this and tell you to go home to your mates," she told me with tears sliding down her face.

I pulled her in for a hug. "I'll bring him home," I told her. "You don't know me yet, but I don't leave people behind."

"I knew I was going to like you," she told me, kissing each side of my face before letting me go.

I continued down the hall to Lewis' office in search of Tessa and a plan.

"Oh, thank heaven, I thought I was going to have to call your mates and tell them I needed their help to find you," Tessa informed me as she wrapped her arms around me in a firm hug.

"I love you too lady and I'm glad you are in one piece," I told her, returning her hug.

"Yeah, Vesper and I got jumped, and by the time I had shit under control, he was nowhere in sight. I was searching for him as well as both you and Lewis when I saw the mass departure of the remaining bad guys. They picked up stakes and portaled out. I didn't see any children, so I thought you guys had found them and brought them here," Tessa explained.

"We found several, and I was bringing them back here while Lewis and Vesper got the last two, but they were attacked, so I immediately ran back through before the portal closed." We got separated when I followed the boy, and they were supposed to meet me inside the tent. They never did. I used my only transport charm to get the three of us back here. But none of the children we found were your niece. I'm sorry."

"That only means we still have work to do," she told me.

Chapter Forty-eight

Raine

"Don't we always?" I asked her sarcastically.

"One day possibly," she deadpanned.

Until that point, I hadn't really looked at my friend. She obviously took a shower, but she was still battered and bruised. I wanted to ask if she was okay but knew she wouldn't appreciate it so instead I asked, "So what's our plan?", sitting down to scarf down my sandwiches.

"First thing I did when I got here, after showering, of course, was to go raid your workshop for everything we might need. I figured it'd save us some time. I was hoping you could do a locator spell to find Lewis first. Then we will find the rest of the kids, my niece included," Tessa told me.

The sound of someone clearing their throat drew our attention to the door. Mrs. Dugan stood in the doorway with the twins in tow.

"They insisted on talking to you ladies before their ride home gets here," she told us.

Walter stepped forward, pulling his twin with him. "My sister heard something when all the people were leaving," he blurted, pushing her towards us. "Tell them, Willy. You don't want what happened to me to happen to them. Do you?"

The girl's lip quivered, and moisture welled in her eye, but she bit down on her bottom lip, seeming to fight past her fear. She looked from us to her brother before finally speaking. "You only have until midnight to find the others. Wally was the test subject and tonight they will do the same thing to the rest of them."

"How do you know?" I asked.

"See, I told you they wouldn't listen Wally. Let's go," Willamina seethed, clearly used to adults not listening because of her age.

I, more than anyone, knew that age meant nothing when it came to the game we call life. Experience mattered, and these kids had been through some things.

Squatting down in front of the girl, so I was at her level, I told her, "I believe you. I was only clarifying, not questioning the truth of what you said."

She looked at her brother and waited for him to nod before answering, "I heard them talking. The powers they are stealing are some kind of payment. That's why they let you find us. We were extras."

After her words, I was the one pissed off. "They were wrong to dismiss you like that. It was their mistake, and we'll use that against them," I told her.

As she and her brother left the office, she nodded once, firmed her jaw, and wiped all traces of the tears from her face.

"You girls go *kick some butt*, as the kids say," Mrs. Dugan told us with a smile before following them.

"Only if those *kids* are on the far side of thirty," Tessa quipped once she was out of hearing range, causing us both to laugh.

"Well, if we are going to do this, we are both going to need to fuel up," I told her, pushing the stack of sandwiches toward her as I went back to munching on my own.

"Speaking of fuel," Tessa said, digging in the bag of supplies she had gathered from my workshop. "Here," she said as she tossed a potion vial my way.

I caught it without a problem. The pale purple flecks in the pink liquid told me it was one of my replenish potions.

"Thank goodness it was one of mine because the ones Liam makes taste like ass," I told her, uncorking it and swallowing it down.

"I'm aware. I told him once I was sure he did it on purpose because no one else's taste that awful," she agreed, tossing hers back as well.

Chapter Forty-nine

Raine

"So, what makes you think we will find them with a tracking spell when we couldn't before?"

"Because they won't expect it. When they thought the kids were our focus, they blocked everyone but you, apparently. Now, hopefully, they will use that same type of spell to hide him," Tessa reasoned.

"And if they have both Lewis and the children blocked. Then what?"

"I'm glad you asked," she told me with an evil grin. "Then we will try Lilly, then Hector. They might be powerful, but you and I both know a spell to block tracking that many people take boatloads of magic. Surely, they can't cover everyone we are looking for all at once."

She had a good theory and with the deadline on the children; we had little to lose by trying.

I grabbed the things I needed from the supplies Tessa had collected while she unrolled the first map, and it began.

Countless maps and most of the supplies later, I had a new thought. I wasn't sure it would work, however with time ticking down I was getting desperate. I grabbed the thermos of Lewis' blood; I'd been saving it until we had a path to take. I wanted to be as strong as possible when the time came to take action.

I quickly gathered the herbs and supplies I would need and a letter opener from the desk. I opened the container of blood and added a few drops to the mix. Even before I ignited the spell with my own blood, the concoction frothed. I pricked my index finger, adding a single drop to activate my enchantment. Purple smoke that I recognized as my magic rolled from the pot until a picture took shape in the air over the desk.

It took several minutes for a picture to form. To my complete and utter surprise, it actually formed two separate visions. The first of the five still missing children. I discovered that they were huddled together in a large cage. They all wore anti-magic collars and, other than appearing dirty, they looked unharmed for the most part. The second was Lewis chained to a wall in the upright position. He had bruises and blood on his body. I couldn't tell from the smokey vision if he was alive or not. Seeing him like that shook something to me.

"This doesn't tell us *where* they are," I seethed. "It's great to see they are all still alive. But how the fuck does this help? We need a-"

"Look!" Tessa exclaimed, pointing to a spot on the map.

"Wait, that's in Damon Cove!" I told her excitedly.

The maps began jumping off the desk until there were only two remaining. One of Damon Cove and one of Farie. Both with glowing orbs.

"And that one is in Farie," Tessa finished.

"Well, that's not ideal. I can't tell which is which. Logic says we go to the closest first, but we need to get the kids before something terrible happens."

"Then I guess we better get our asses in gear," Tessa stated, already loading her pockets with potions and knives.

Tessa had a small amount of magic, but she was a killer shot with knives, swords, anything with a blade was her jam.

Since we were heading out, I downed the rest of Lewis' blood. It was like mainlining a pot of espresso. I had never felt as strong as I did at that moment. I could feel every molecule of water in the air. The blood in my veins sang with a power I hadn't felt before. I'd felt the same magic on a much smaller scale when I was using water to freeze Willamina's iron cuffs. I experimented by trying to pool the water into my palm, but the thought created a ball of water the size of a basketball in the air between Tessa and me.

"That's a new trick," Tessa said, staring at the ball of water.

"Yeppers." I would have liked to question the development of a new power when I should have been losing them. But there would be time once everyone was safe.

Chapter Fifty

Raine

Thankfully, Tessa was a far sight better at reading a map than I was because I was most definitely shit at it. We took the bikes and left Mr. and Mrs. Dugan on standby with the van, in case we found the kids first. Not that our hopes were high that it would be the children who were local. It made more sense for them to bring Lewis here than the children. Since four of the five still missing children were fae, it was logical to think that was where they would have taken them. But we wanted to be fast and able to transverse most terrains without issue. Which proved to be a good plan when the trail led onto the back roads of the Georgia swamp.

We drove down the red clay road; the night air was warm and moist and would have been pleasant if not for the countdown clock in my head telling me we were running out of time. Tessa stopped at the end of the path we'd been following.

"I think we should hoof it from here. We don't want to announce our arrival," she told me, dismounting the bike and triggering the shrinking spell before placing it in her pocket.

I followed her lead. Listening for anything that did not belong.

We entered the swamp on foot, about a mile from our first target. Three months ago, that would have tested my physicality. Now, I didn't even feel out of breath. Likely because I no longer needed to breathe.

We were still about a quarter of a mile away from our target when I felt the foul magic. It felt like fire ants devouring my skin. By the time we were close enough for me to hear the chanting. There was something dark underway and if we didn't get a move on, I had an awful feeling that it would be too late.

Tessa must have felt something as well, because she doubled her speed. Once we were close enough to see the glow of their magic, we slowed to a stop far enough away that they weren't likely to feel any spells I performed.

"Thoughts?"

"I was about to ask you the same thing," Tessa replied, while keeping her head on a swivel, looking for threats while we brainstormed.

I had no military training. However, in my short time since discovering the supernatural world was real, I'd been in constant battles. A lesser woman would undoubtedly have gone running like her ass was on fire even with the stunning mates. It could be brutal. But that wasn't me. Since the moment I'd learned who I was, I'd become a different woman.

While I hated to admit it, we both knew the best course of action would be to split up. Though, splitting up last time was why we were standing there two men down.

"I think we should stay together until we are close enough to see how many we are dealing with. Then we separate."

"But keep each other in line of sight," Tessa finished for me.

"You know it," I quipped in a low tone.

The Georgia night was crisp and growing cool as we trudged through the Georgia pines, hemlock, and white oak trees, strung with Spanish moss. It wasn't long before we were able to see what we were up against.

The forest opened up into an unnatural clearing. Trees ringed the open area with the children as a central point positioned at each point of a pentagram. The five remaining children each stood at the points of the pentagram. Around them stood ten bad guys, two to each child. There appeared to only be three that were magic users. Whether they were witches or mage I couldn't say for sure. There were also four demons. The remaining three were shifters: none of them smelled like wolves, possibly bear by their scent.

Tessa motioned to the right and headed left. Before she could take a step, I reached out and stopped her. Muttering a few words of Latin, I placed a protection spell over her. It wouldn't be as effective as if we were touching, so I could constantly feed power into it, but it'd be better than nothing. I didn't want to lose my one remaining ally.

"Signal when you are in place. We will attack from opposite sides."

"I guess I'll take the five on the left. The five on the right are all yours," Tessa retorted.

After that, she dissolved into the cover of the forest. With her hair the color of the night sky and wearing dark tactical gear, she was a blur of shadow as she moved.

I picked my way through the woods. The only source of light came from torches outside the outer circle. Thankfully, my vampire and wolf genes seemed to work together, so I could see very well. There were three girls and two boys. I'd never met Tessa's niece, so I had no clue which one she was. Though they all appeared unharmed at that moment, which I took as a win.

Chapter Fifty-one

Raine

I'd reached the halfway point and was waiting for the go ahead from Tessa when one girl began screaming, followed by a second. I could finally see the spell they were weaving, and it was beyond dark. Shadows danced and coalesced in the torchlight, sucking away what little light there was. Shadow beast stalked the area just beyond the weak light. The more that poured into the space, the cooler the night air became.

It wasn't until the third girl added her voice to the howls that Tessa finally signaled, but she was already on the move heading for the assailant closest to her. She tackled one while throwing a dagger at another. Her blade struck center mass. The one she tackled was attempting to transform. She slammed a second blade into his heart and tossed a fireball at a third all before I took ten steps.

Not wanting to be outdone I kicked my ass into high gear. I threw an energy ball at the shadow beasties and the first bad guy I saw while knocking a second's legs out from under him with a stream of water then followed up with a kick to the head, before transforming my hands so I could use my claws to rip out his throat.

I felt the spell heading my way a second before it hit. Thanks to my new vampire speed, I could sidestep the worst of it. As a result of the spell, my left side was struck, causing me to fall to the ground and fracturing both my humerus and a couple of ribs. The pain slowed my movements, allowing a panther shifter to get the jump on me. The cat chomped down on my calf, yanking me off my feet again. I went down hard, jarring the new fractures. I bit back a moan as tears sprang to my eyes.

I stabbed my claws into his snout, but he still didn't release my leg. He thrashed his head from side to side, attempting to tear the flesh from my body. Every shake of his head ground bone on bone in my arm, as wave after wave of pain crashed over me, causing dark spots to dance in my periphery. I attempted to kick him in the head, except the angle was wrong, so there was no power behind it.

A second big cat came at my face. I sunk my claw into its eye. It popped like an overripe grape. The shifter gave an inhuman yawl before shifting back to his human form. Blood poured from the empty socket and the optic nerve hung down his cheek. The eyeball a slimy, deflated balloon dangling from the end. He writhed on the grass, alternating between cursing and crying. If I hadn't been hyped up on adrenaline, I would likely have puked.

I climbed to my feet, still hunched over with pain, counting the second until my healing could repair the damage. Bodies littered the ground but two of the magic users continued working the spell. Two of the children were no longer standing. I said a silent prayer. They were alright as I shambled towards the closer of the two still casting, throwing my strongest spells in rapid succession.

The closer of them, a tall red head with a pixie cut, stumbled falling to one knee, breaking the connection. Three of the kids ran but the fourth, a girl with dark hair, was trying to get the two girls off the ground and away from the pentagram. She wasn't having much luck, however the second caster, a short potbelly, balding man, was taking aim at her and the red head was back on her feet, I didn't have time to focus on her task. I needed to keep them both off her, to give her time to help the others.

I threw a knife at the redhead. The blade sank hilt deep in the center of the abdomen. It severed her abdominal aorta, killing her before she even hit the grass. Taking aim at the fat man next. He noticed the others were down and he ran. I pushed down the desire to check on the girls and gave chase.

He was fast for a man his size, but I was faster. I was four steps behind him when he entered the tree line. Two steps later, an avalanche of pain knocked me off my feet. An arrow protruded from my right knee. I reached down to break it off so I could remove it easier. I was yanked up by my neck. An arm was around my throat and secured against a firm chest. He was taller than I was, causing my feet to dangle several inches above the ground.

Lewis had told me multiple times that breathing, now that I was a vampire, wasn't necessary. Logically, I knew he was right. I had died and resurrected. Yet as I hung there suspended, gasping like a fish in sand, my brain still refused to believe it, fight or flight be damned.

Chapter Fifty-two

Raine

Flashes of darkness danced at the edges of my field of vision again, and my body felt heavy and weightless all at the same time. I wanted to continue fighting. I wanted to overpower my brain with its human ideology.

That ideology must have stopped me from struggling long enough that he thought I had passed out or died because his hold relaxed fractionally. My feet hit the ground, and I took the only action my addled brain could think of. I sank my shiny new fangs into his beefy arm and ripped.

He was a demon, so his blood tasted like ash and fish of the rotten variety. I gagged as he screamed and dragged me down with him when someone knocked his feet out from under him. I stabbed my last dagger into his leg as I rolled away. As I yanked it from his upper thigh with a twist and a jerk, I left him bleeding out, severing his femoral artery.

He turned to ash and his body drifted away as Tessa helped me to my feet.

"Shit girl, I leave you for five minutes and you nearly get yourself choked out. What the hell?" she demanded.

"You were taking so long I got bored. Had to find something to do while I waited," I deadpanned, looking around for the last of the bad guys. He was gone, and I didn't see any signs of others.

She pulled out her cell phone and dialed without replying. I walked slowly toward where the children stood at the edge of the clearing. I took my time not wanting to traumatize them any more than they had already been, and the fact was they did not know me.

Thankfully, Tessa was off the phone quickly and joined me when I was still several yards away.

"Rosemary and Victor will meet us at the road to pick up the kids in about fifteen minutes, then we will use a transportation charm to get to Farie. If luck is on our side, maybe we can be in bed by dawn," she stated as we walked.

The girl that I'd seen earlier trying to help the girl that hadn't been able to run away stepped away from the others as we approached.

"How are they holding up?" Tessa asked her as she pulled her into a hug.

"Bae's powers aren't currently working, which has her freaked out, but they're still there. They're just weak," she stated matter-of-factly. She already had her aunt's spine of steel and no-nonsense attitude.

"What have I told you about others and their feelings?" her aunt asked.

"That just because that's not how I feel doesn't mean I should discount them," she stated sullenly.

"Suma say hello to my friend Raine," Tessa told her niece, "Raine my niece Suma, who is still learning how to not judge others," she said to me.

"She's kind of famous auntie Tae," the girl said to Tessa. Then she turned to me. "It's very nice to meet you, even if it's only after getting kidnapped."

"Suma!" Tessa barked.

"What? It's the truth!" she told her aunt indignantly.

"I'm aware. Please excuse her, Raine. She's-"

I laughed as I interrupted Tessa and said, "You're right, Suma. I'm sorry I didn't get to meet you until after you were kidnapped. But I'm happy to meet you now. Kidnapping aside... In my defense, I've only been around a few months," I told her with a smile.

"That's okay. I don't blame you. I blame Auntie Tae. She knows my friends and I have a bet going on who would get to meet you first. If I win, she will do my homework for a week," she informed me.

"Suma!" Tessa scolded, "That's cheating!"

"No, cheating is if I copy her work. If she does it and I hand it in, that's forgery at best," she quipped.

"What does she get if she wins?" I had to ask.

She looked from Tessa to me and back before answering, "Since I met you first, it's a moot point."

"Touche," was the only answer I had. She was clearly smart as a tack, but I felt sorry for her parents. I had a feeling she was going to cause them both gray hair. Yet I doubted they'd want her to be any other way.

Chapter fifty-three

Lewis

It wasn't long before it was apparent that my inability to hear anything was because of a spell. Keeping prisoners from communicating with each other was only one of the reasons for a spell such as that. The other being for the psychological benefits. Leave someone in the dark with no sound and nothing to focus on and the average person will do or say anything to escape in no time.

Too bad for my jailer. I didn't have any intention to do anything average. Of course, my friendly neighborhood captor wasn't of the average variety, either. Aside from when several of them suspended me from the wall, there had only been one.

He and I used *him,* because of the person's size, since they were also using an obfuscation spell to hide their identity, as they used my body as a punching bag for hours. The thing was, he never asked a question. In fact, he hadn't uttered a single solitary word the entire time.

He just pummeled my body, took a break, and began again. Whoever he was, he knew how to slow my natural healing ability and took pleasure in allowing enough time between beatings for the splits in my skin to re-knit together before he pummeled me again to reopen them. It was an altogether unpleasant game of lather, rinse, repeat.

I must have blacked out because when I regained consciousness, I was alone. Unlike the previous times, someone had left the door open and hadn't reengaged the silence spell.

From the sounds filtering into my lovely abode, I could tell there were others nearby. Be they captor or jailer, I could not be sure. What I knew was that I needed to figure out how to get the hell off the wall I was suspension from and find out if the others were also residents of Hotel Torture.

My father would never let me forget it if my brother got injured while helping me complete a task that he had assigned me to complete.

The problem was dangling as I was in iron cuffs didn't give me much range of motion in my legs. The one thing going for me was the shackles I wore were also iron. However, the links were long enough to allow a small amount of movement and the anchor holding my arms had loosened with the repeated beatings and my weight. I spent more time than I care to admit getting myself turned around and positioned well enough to leverage myself in a way to use my weight to loosen it further.

A punch to the kidney was my first clue he had returned. I couldn't turn around to face him, however, this time he spoke, so there was no need. It was the last voice I thought I'd heard.

Chapter fifty-four

Raine

The Dugans showed up to pick up the five remaining children, and it only took Tessa five minutes of arguing and a promise of cookies to get Suma into the van. The girl was a mini version of her aunt down to the stubborn set of her chin when things weren't going her way and, with her negotiation skills, I could easily see her following her into the field of law as well.

"She is so hardheaded," Tessa seethed. "I have no clue where she gets it. Her mother is the sweetest person you could ever meet, and my brother is a teddy bear."

"Don't you?"

"Ha, ha... You know you aren't half as funny as you think, right?" she deadpanned.

I smiled, but kept my mouth shut.

Tessa was the one who had a general idea of where Lewis was being held. We had agreed to transport to an area a mile away from where he was being held. And he obviously had to have been being held against his will, otherwise he would have found us.

The forest we arrived in was completely different from the one we had left in Georgia. The grass was so green it vibrated with health and vitality. Why I could feel grass was beyond me, however, since I'd never been to Farie, nor had I ever been whatever I was becoming. Because even I knew my transition wasn't going like Lewis' had or how he thought it would.

That fact was driven home when the tree I was standing next to snaked out a limb and caressed my arm.

"Well, that's new," Tessa quipped, looking from me to the tree and back.

"Yep, my life seems to be all about *new* lately."

"You'll figure it out. If you haven't let the shit you've been through thus far get you down, a few new powers sure won't," she told me.

"That's true," I admitted with a smile.

What she failed to mention was that she and my girls helped me handle everything that had been thrown at me with ease. None of them judged me or my past. They gave only understanding. It was a rare thing in a world full of people who only thought about themselves to find friends that would not only support you, but call you on your shit.

I followed Tessa as she headed toward our target. Thankfully, no other trees reached out to say hello, and I focused on finding Lewis and, hopefully, Vesper. Then that still left Lilly and Hector to find, and I was hoping they were all in the same place.

We were still about a quarter of a mile from our destination when I finally sensed his presence. We were still about a quarter of a mile from where we were headed when I finally *felt* him. Until that point, I hadn't let myself think about the *what ifs* where Lewis was concerned. In the first few moments after I felt him, I was so stunned I nearly tripped over my own feet with relief.

"He's close," I told Tessa in a hushed tone.

"Lewis? You can feel him or whatever?" she asked, slowing our pace as she searched the trees for anything out of the normal.

"Of course, Lewis. Who else?"

Chapter fifty-Five

Raine

Movement twenty paces in front of us stalled any further conversation. We ducked behind a large boulder as two wolf shifters walked past.

"Should we follow them?" I asked once they were far enough away. I felt it was safe.

"Oh definitely," Tessa replied.

We followed at a good distance, letting them lead us through the forest until the area opened into a glen that abutted a cliff. The men we were trailing disappeared behind a large boulder, so I readied a stunner spell and handed Tessa a sleeping potion, as well as a potion bomb, in case we got separated again. She had fire, acid and was one of the toughest hand to hand combatants I'd ever seen, hell I'd seen her put men twice her size on their ass more times than I cared to count, still I didn't want to lose track of her even if she could handle herself. Something told me she was in danger if we got separated. Which sounded stupid, since she had handled herself fine when she and Vesper were attacked.

We crept closer then their voices faded. The boulder hid a path leading down the cliff into an open cave. There were several spells on the opening, but I was able to make quick work of them. With all the magic that had been used up to that point, it was laughable how low-level they were.

"What's wrong?" Tessa asked as I stood searching for any unseen spells or traps I may have missed.

"The spells, they are too simple."

"And that's a bad thing?" she asked, staying alert.

"Normally no, however, something feels... Off."

"So, do you want to turn around?" she asked.

"No. This is where Lewis is being held. I'm sure of it, and I don't think we are going to find another way in."

"Do you think it's a trap?" Tess inquired.

"Oh, definitely."

"Oh, I see. It's like that," she mocked, tucking the potion bottles into her jacket pocket and pulling out two daggers instead.

"Why does it feel like you are having fun?"

"Because you know me. Of course!" she replied with an evil smile.

I was very glad to have her on my side as we stepped into the dark cave. The cave wasn't over fifteen feet wide and deep.

The floor sloped to the back, and I was very thankful for my vampire sight as we descended into the depths of the fae realm.

The cave narrowed to the point we were required to walk single file to proceed. I took the lead. We walked silently until we noticed glowing ahead.

"Do you hear anything?" Tess whispered next to my ear.

"No, but I can smell blood. Lewis and several others, both old and new."

"Noted," she replied.

The tunnel curved to the right before widening. There were two heavy metal doors on one side and three on the other. Which was where the scent of both the old and new blood originated from, Lewis' among them.

The first two were unlocked and empty. What we found in the third was gut wrenching.

Chapter fifty-six

Raine

Hector and Lily both hung limply in manacles from the far cave wall. The cell had some sort of glowing fireless torch allowing us to easily see the dried blood matting Lily's hair through the opening in the door, but not enough to see much else. Like whether either of them was still breathing. Tessa called out in a low tone. Neither of them moved.

I pulled a potion bomb from my stash and added a few additional herbs and a dash of fire magic and presto, change-o, and you had magic acid that could melt a foot of tungsten in two point five seconds. Tessa swung the door open, and I did a quick search for spells before we stepped into the cell. Getting us trapped in the cell with them wouldn't be helpful when we were so close to Lewis.

I could feel him like an extra limb, just out of reach. He was so close; it took everything I had not to ditch Tessa and hunt until I found him.

Lily moaned and Tessa rushed to where she dangled with her arms above her head, toes just skimming the floor. Since she had Lily, I checked on Hector. He was breathing, but in bad shape. His left jaw was fractured. Both of his eyes were swollen, nearly shut, with a gash across the bridge of his nose.

Lily moaned again, trailed by a curse from Tessa.

"Here, give her this healing potion. If you can get it down her, it will help with the pain while it's healing her." I may have been new to the magical world, however, it hadn't taken long to figure out that traditionally potions did a single thing. Healing potions healed while doing nothing to ease the person's pain. While pain relief potions relieved pain, yet did nothing to repair or fix the cause of the pain.

When someone was injured, they might need to take several potions to address each symptom.

"A combination potion? You can do that?" Tessa asked, already holding the vial to Lily's lips.

"Yeah. I've been playing with a few variations. Not all have been successful. This, however, is some of my best so far."

"Still tastes like shit," Lily muttered through swollen lips. There was a large cut to her bottom lip that was already beginning to heal.

"Yeah, unfortunately everything I try to do to improve it decreases the effectiveness. Sorry."

"And it is effective. My teeth feel numb, and my brain is floaty," Lily stated dreamily. "I will deal with the taste as long as it feels like this."

A guttural moan quashed my desire to laugh. The hair on my arms stood on end and my heart stuttered in my chest. My feet were moving before the thought had even formed to do so.

I followed the moans to find the man I'd wanted to throttle nearly every minute since meeting him. He had been controlling, rude, dismissive and an all-around discomfort in my nether region. I guess the song really was true when it said *you're going to miss me when I'm gone.*

I rushed to the battered and bloody form staked to the cave wall. The man was hardly recognizable as the sexy broody Fae-Vampire known as Lewis Damon.

He mumbled something. At least I thought he did, but with the damage to his face, I couldn't be sure, so I concentrated on setting him free. It sucked that I was becoming quite efficient at removing iron cuffs. It didn't, however, help calm my nerves. My heart continued to gallop at a rapid rate, making my palms sweat. I fought off the feeling of dread that things were going too smoothly and prayed things wouldn't go tits up.

Lewis moaned again, and I noticed his fangs had been yanked out. Anger shot through my very soul, fueling my magic as I shot a stream of water and dropped the temperature around the iron to freeze the shackle before ramming my fist into the metal, shattering the cuff securing his left wrist. His arm hung limply. It was clearly dislocated. There wasn't a spot on the man that hadn't sustained some type of damage. Steeling myself, I repeated the process on his left ankle. I hadn't planned it out very well and with Lewis so weak and injured, removing the restraints was causing his weight to reopen several of the wounds, the worst of which was a gaping hole in his lower abdomen.

Fresh blood leaked from the area.

"Shit, shit, double shit," I muttered as I used my dagger to slice the sleeve from my shirt so I could press it to the wound as I dug my last healing potion from my pocket. While trying to recall if my single high school anatomy class taught me which of the vital organs were located in the right lower abdomen.

It took several attempts to uncork the bottle. By the time I got the potion to his lips, my hands were trembling so badly I dribbled the first few drops on his chin as I attempted to pour it into his mouth.

As I stood on my toes holding his chin, to keep his mouth shut, waiting for him to swallow, my eyes burned, and my vision blurred as tears leaked down my cheeks. I don't know when or how it had happened, but at some point, I had fallen for the grumpy pain in the ass and I couldn't imagine a world without him in it. It was too depressing.

Chapter fifty-seven

Raine

An eternity later, his throat finally bobbed as he swallowed the potion. I was never so happy to see a man's throat move in all my life. Time stomped by at a snail's pace as I waited for his eyes to open.

The scuff of movement behind me pulled me from my wait. I spun with an energy ball in hand. There was no immediate source of the sound until the sound repeated, at which time I noted movement in the shadows of the cell. I noticed the third person in the cell. They were little more than a heap in the darkness.

"Raine?"

At the croak of my name, I turned to where Lewis dangled from the manacles still securing his right arm and legs to the wall.

I was torn between investigating the threat and throwing my arms around his neck. He saved me the decision when he used his recently healed left arm to pull me to him and claimed my lips in the gentlest of kisses. It was but a whisper of a touch. Still, it stole the breath from my lungs.

"Wh-what was that for?" I mumbled, trying to shake off the euphoric flush the mere touch of his lips had created.

"Just making sure you were real," he told me with a loopy smile.

"Obviously, the pain relief of that healing potion is working. I'm going to finish getting you the rest of the way off this wall. Then we need to check out what's moving around over there in the corner," I told Lewis as I worked on removing the last two cuffs.

"That won't be necessary." The voice was the last I'd expected, but I couldn't say I was sorry.

"Good to see-" my words were cut off as I was yanked off balance when Lewis shoved me between him and the wall.

"That was rather rude, brother. The lady went through all the trouble of saving you for you to go pushing her around. I'm rather certain that women don't care for that type of behavior. Here, let's ask another of your ladies," Vesper stated.

He pulled Lily in front of him where he stood in the cell's doorway. Her face held fresh bruises, as did her neck. It wasn't until this point that I put the pieces together. Which frankly pissed me the hell off.

"I see you are *finally* putting things together," Vesper stated in a snide tone. "And here I was worried you'd been on to me when you refused to fall for my charms."

"Nah, sleazy just doesn't do it for me," I replied.

He ignored my reply and continued talking like a typical villain performing his final monologue. "You were the perfect pawn, you know. Your actions exceeded my expectations," he exclaimed, clearly delighted. You have no clue about the trouble it took for me to find just the right combination of partners to carry out my plans. Then you came along playing Nancy Drew with my brother all focused on you. It was almost too easy. Thank you, by the way, for disposing of those partners. They weren't very pleased that you returned all those kids, keeping them from all that power. With them all dead problems solved," he boasted.

"Trust me, it wasn't for your benefit!" I barked, my anger getting the better of me. I hated myself for thinking my unease around him had been because of his general skeeviness instead of my inner warning system. Trusting myself was still something I was working on.

"Worked in my favor, that's all that matters," he continued.

"Why? What could you have needed so bad that it was worth harming innocent children?"

"Power, of course," he stated, as if it should be obvious.

"Being the next king isn't enough?" I asked.

"There's the rub, as they say. Next, *If... If* my father doesn't change his mind. *Should he decide to step down? If* I do as I'm told. *Assuming I abide by the rules.* If! If! If! I'm so damn tired of the never-ending list of ifs. I really thought when he disowned my brother that he would finally see me. That he would finally get out of my way. Then he goes all soft and threatens to name Lewis as heir again. After all, I did to get him out of my way. Damn incompetent vampire. Useless the whole of them. But thanks for your help. Without you, I might not have been able to spend all the quality time with my family," he said with a chuckle.

Lewis gave my hand a squeeze as I stepped from behind him. At one time, I might have believed his words. I was no longer that person and if he believed I was, he was wrong; I was not a pawn. I was a goddamn queen, and I was going to show him just what it was to mess with me and mine.

As Vesper spoke, he stepped into the cell and passed Lily to a minion. I met Lewis' gaze and hoped he would follow my lead.

The sound of movement behind Vesper gave me the opening I needed. I took three steps, dropped to my knees and grabbed a handful of his crown and family jewels, if you know what I mean, and twisted for all I was worth. When he dropped to his knees howling, I followed up with a kick to his face, planning to scour my hand at my earliest convenience.

Tessa had the minion in a choke hold while Lily held up Hector. He leaned heavily on her as the open fracture to his right leg continued to heal.

She passed me iron cuffs to secure him, which I did before asking no one in particular, "What the fuck is he talking about?"

"That is a bit of a story," croaked a voice from the shadows in the corner.

Chapter fifty-eight

Raine

The unknown voice had us all reaching for weapons and spells.

"It really would be regrettable if my saviors were also my executioners," the voice stated matter-of-factly.

"Father?" Lewis asked hesitantly, stepping forward.

"Affirmative, though after your brother's behavior as of late, I'm wondering about that choice," he croaked.

I created a couple of light orbs and tossed them in the air as Lewis helped his father up from where he lay on the ground. Like his son, he was battered and bruised, though not nearly as badly. Unfortunately for him, I had no more healing potions. Thankfully, he didn't appear to have any fractures, so I gave him my final pain elixir.

"Here, take this. I'm out of healing potions, but this will help with your pain."

He took the vial, uncorked it, and downed it in one large gulp. After several moments, his breathing became less labored, the tension in his frame relaxed, and he stood straighter.

"That is quite effective. Without the iron he's been restraining me with, my natural healing should repair the majority of my injuries by tomorrow. Thank you for your kindness after the way I treated you," he told me.

I wasn't sure exactly what to say. "You are welcome. It appears that my emotions are heightened since my transition. Who knew becoming a vampire was so emotional?" I joked.

"Indeed," he responded, clearly missing the sarcasm.

Lewis assisted his father as we made our way from the caves. Apparently, the cave walls were full of iron ore, which prevented Lewis from creating a portal. After we were outside, he opened a portal to his father's castle.

It was a literal castle, the only thing missing was a mote. As soon as we exited the portal, Lewis' father called several guards to take Vesper to the dungeon. As much as I wanted to follow and make sure they rammed him into as many walls as possible along the way I stayed.

Tessa stayed back with me as Lewis led his father to his office. He asked a woman dressed in a blue peasant style dress to fetch a healer for both his father and Hector. Hector was still leaning heavily on Lily, so it was a good idea.

"Did you want to follow them to the dungeon and shove him down a flight of stairs or six? Or was that just me projecting?" Tessa whispered.

"My idea was walls, but only because I wasn't sure if steps were available to push him down," I told her, making us both laugh.

Lewis looked back and gave us an odd look. One of those *what the hell woman* looks, however, the slight smirk made me smile.

I wasn't sure when, but at some point, the uptight, no-nonsense, cold-hearted vamp had grown on me.

Chapter fifty-nine

Lewis

When I opened my eyes to find Raine in my cell attempting to free me, I thought it was a hallucination. Yet as soon as my lips touched hers, my battered and beaten body sparked to life. I felt like a still heart, and she was the defibrillator I needed to jump start me.

Even with all the damage my brother had inflicted on my body, I wanted her. Right there, right then. I wasn't sure when she had wormed her way in, but she had.

All the quirks that should drive me insane, like her penchant for doing the exact opposite of what she was told, while always putting others first. Even to her own detriment. The thing was, her defiance had led us to where we were. With all the children's home safe and sound, and the bad guy behind bars. Hell, she even saved me when she could have left and returned to her mates. How could I be mad about that?

I helped my father to his office. While he still lived in the castle, our family had built it thousands of years ago. He at least didn't use the throne room as his base of operations. He had thankfully given that up years ago. Not that his office was any less opulent. His desk was Amazon Rosewood and the stained glass window behind it highlighted the rich reds, oranges, pinks and violets in the wood's grain. The plush chairs and settee were pale chestnut leather.

I sat next to Raine on the settee as the healer took care of the worst of my father's injuries, even though he had tried to brush her off. However, Marigold, his personal healer, wouldn't hear of allowing him to heal naturally, king or not. She then healed Hector's leg, though the healing draft he'd taken had him nearly healed. As soon as she left the room, closing the door behind her, Raine turned to my father expectantly.

"I'm sure you can understand Vesper's jealousy towards Luwianos. As the firstborn, he was the heir, and as the second son, Vesper was only a prince. When he was younger, that was enough. As he got older, it became the cause of every issue between the two. The fact that Luwianos did not wish to rule only made Vesper's resentment grow. I was unaware how much." He explained. "Over the years, that resentment grew until he took matters into his own hands."

"So, this wasn't his first stunt like this?" Raine demanded.

"Unfortunately, no. This is, however, the worst to date," he admitted.

"Forgive my bluntness, but plenty of second born royalty are jealous and they do not kidnap small children to steal their powers. Nor do they attempt to break every bone in their older brother's body just to secure a throne said brother already lost," she stated bluntly.

When father merely sat there, I answered for him.

"He was making another power play. He was tired of waiting for father to step down and allow him to rule."

"Another? What was the first?" Natessa asked, glancing from me to my father and back.

"It appears the attack that left me a vampire was his first."

"He had you made into a vampire so he could have the crown?" Raine demanded.

"You weren't supposed to transition," Natessa supplied. "That explains why you were left like you were. I'm going to kick his ass!" she shouted, surging to her feet.

"And I'm going to help her," Raine declared, surging to her feet. Her claws were out, and her pale hair danced in an invisible breeze. The fire in her eyes promised a slow, painful experience for my brother if she was ever allowed near him.

"Vesper will face punishment for his crimes. All of his crimes," father stated in his kingly tone.

Their anger on my behalf warmed my tiny, cold heart.

Chapter sixty

Raine

I had believed that I hated Vesper for his involvement in kidnapping those innocent children and torturing Lewis and the others, but when I heard that he caused Lewis' transformation, a rage ignited within me I had never experienced before. Hearing his father, who had allowed Vesper to become the power obsessed asshole who had attempted to not only steal children's powers but kill both his brother and father as well, didn't instill confidence.

"How exactly will he pay?"

"I'm not able to say," Lewis' father replied.

Lewis explained before I bit his father's head off, which upon reflection might have been ill advised since he was king after all, and we were in his kingdom.

"The council will decide after hearing his list of crimes. His punishment could be anything from imprisonment to the stripping of his powers," he explained.

"Shouldn't he be sentenced to both, at the very least? He took Walter's powers, and he tried to have you killed. Luckily, he hired an inept vampire for the task and when that didn't work, he still wasn't happy and beat not only you but your father, Lily, and Hector. Having his powers stripped should be a given after all he's done." I was growling by the end of my rant.

It wasn't until Lewis clasp my hand in his that I noticed my hands. My claws were extended, which wasn't unusual. However, they were also covered in iridescent blue-green scales.

"What the hell?" I demanded, jumping from the chair, while shaking out my hands like I could shake off the scales.

Tessa jumped to her feet, pulling knives from somewhere as she searched for the danger.

"It's alright," Lewis told me in a calming manner.

"It obviously is not! I! Have! Scales!" I screeched, still shaking my hands, even though it was obviously doing nothing to dispel them.

"And it won't," his father stated matter-of-factly.

"Say more words," I shrieked.

"You're a shifter. You know that the more heightened your emotions the more difficult it is to shift. Right?" he asked serenely, as if I weren't having more changes than a teen boy during puberty.

Which only served to piss me off more. I'd quickly decided I didn't care for the man. Even if I did have sympathy for what he'd suffered at his youngest son's hand. But any father who denied his son his birthright over something that was out of his control, even if he didn't want it, wasn't worthy of a son like Lewis.

After several minutes Lewis took both my scaly hands in his. "Breath... in through your nose... out, through your mouth."

It took several rounds of him doing so with me, but finally, with his calming mantra, the scales melted slowly back into my skin. Which freaked me out almost as much as the dragon skin had.

"Better?" he asked after several minutes had passed without the scales reappearing.

"I think so."

"Now father, what is it that you know about Raine's problem with her powers?" Lewis asked.

Chapter sixty-one

Raine

It took entirely too long for his father to reply for my liking. Of course, my claws digging into Lewis' hand were the only thing that kept me from attempting to strangle the answers from his father. Well, that and the dried blood still caked on his skin and clothes, the only evidence of the damage his youngest son had done.

"I admit that when I first met you, I was intrigued. My son has only ever brought home two females in all his years. The first was Lily, who has no living relatives and has been like a daughter to him. The second was you, the opposite of her. So, I looked at you. More precisely, your genealogy."

Before I could tell him what exactly I thought of that in a loud volume, likely involving many colorful curse words, he continued.

"At first glance, it would seem your heritage was a witch with a shifter hybrid here and there. Though without adding vampire and fae blood to the mix, they likely never knew what your true potential could be. You see, what few people know is that when you have the right combination of supernatural DNA, something extraordinary can happen. I believe this is what you are experiencing," he explained.

"Okay, so something in my DNA is allowing me to do what? What's going on with me?"

"Something truly exceptional," he stated.

When I growled in response, he continued, "I think when you ingested my son's blood, you collected the remaining two genes you needed, vampire and fae. I believe you are now what is known as a chimera."

"Meaning what?"

"Meaning you can collect powers and use them as your own."

"I collect other supernatural powers? Like I steal them or something?"

"Not steal, more mimic them permanently," he explained.

"I guess that's better," I mumbled suddenly, exhausted. "So, I'm not a vampire?"

"Of that I am unsure," he told me.

"We'll figure it out, sweetie. Right Lewis?" Tessa said, patting my hand reassuringly.

Lewis had remained silent throughout his father's explanation.

"Are there others?" he asked in lieu of a response.

"Not that I'm aware of," his father told him.

"How long has it been since there was another?" Lewis asked.

"None in the last five hundred years that I'm aware of," he stated.

Lewis gave a single nod before standing and heading toward the door. "I assume the council will rule in seven days?"

Once his father nodded, he continued, "Then we will be present for the ruling, as will the families of the children," he told his father, and left without waiting for a response or to see if the rest of us would follow.

Chapter sixty-two

Lewis

I knew before asking, yet I had to anyway. "How long has it been since there was another?"

"None in the last five hundred years that I'm aware of," father confirmed.

A thousand more questions were parading through my mind, yet one look at the fear and uncertainty on Raine's face told me it wasn't the time to seek those answers.

"I assume the council will rule in seven days?"

When he nodded in agreement I left after adding, "Then we will be present for the ruling, as will the families of the children," I told him without waiting for a response and exited without giving a shit what he had to say on the matter.

I felt every one of my one hundred and fifty years as I opened a portal back to Damon Cove. We exited on the front lawn as the sun was rising.

"Am I the only one who needs a drink?" Natessa asked as she climbed the three steps to the wrap-around porch and headed inside without waiting for an answer.

The porch was one reason I bought the house. The other was the stretch of white sand behind it. It would never be the coasts of Fairie, but it also did not come with the burdens either.

My feet drifted toward the beach as the blazing red, orange, and gold of the sun reflected off the dark waves. When I reached the sand, I removed my socks and shoes so I could walk at the water's edge, allowing the waves to lap at my feet.

While I walked, I thought about what the coming days would hold. Once the council delivered Vesper's sentence, there'd be no valid reason to continue to keep Raine with me. She had shown remarkable ability to handle whatever was thrown her way. After the ruling was rendered, I could help her seek out to help with her new powers or someone to help her learn to hide them. It was her choice. I'd support her either way. Though I'd have to do so from a distance, I couldn't hold her hostage any longer, as much as I might want to. She had a life and mates to get back to and while my reasons for bringing her to my realm had been valid. She had proven she could handle her vampire side. Plus, who knew what my future held once Vesper's punishment was delivered? Even if they didn't strip him of his powers after what he did to the children, there was no way the people would allow him to become king. Since our family line consisted of my father, Vesper, and I, the council could elect to name the head of the second founding family as ruler if they so chose.

I was only head of Damon Cove because it allowed those like me who didn't fit in to have a place to call home. It allowed the weaker supernaturals a measure of safety they wouldn't have otherwise. Which had been what I needed when I gave up trying to convince Lily she needed to be with a family. After she ran away from family number three, I let her stay. Damon Cove had given her a true place to grow up. One day, my hope was that Lily would want to take my place. If she didn't, I would find someone else when that time came.

I had just turned around to head back when the dulcet tones of Raine's voice shook me from my musings.

"A penny for your thoughts," she offered.

"Just attempting to organize my thoughts before I meet with the children's families. As happy as I'm sure they must be to have their children back, I imagine they are eager for answers."

"I'd like to tag along if you think that would be alright?" she asked.

"I think that would be nice."

Chapter sixty-three

Raine

Why I had followed Lewis as he walked up the beach, I couldn't have said until he turned to head back towards the house. The look on his face was anything but the cold creature I had believed him to be. His was the face of a man who carried the weight of a ruler. Not the kind of ruler Vesper would have been, but the kind Lucian's mother and father were. The type I strived to become.

Of course, the smirky smile he gave me when I offered, "A penny for your thoughts," was worth the shock. Though when he answered and allowed me to carry part of the burden, even a small measure, had the feelings that had been growing where he was concerned rampaging.

It shouldn't have surprised me that he was thinking about what to say to the parents of the children who had been kidnapped. That *he* would want to speak to them personally.

"We should probably shower, then eat before we head to town," he suggested.

I'm not even a little embarrassed to admit in that half second between the word *shower* and *then* that I was hoping he was suggesting something sexy. When he didn't, I reminded myself that wasn't where my brain should be and followed him back to the house. I'm not ashamed to admit I enjoyed the view as I did.

Lewis was sitting at the kitchen bar in a pair of faded jeans and a gray henley, sipping a cup of green tea, when I finished my shower. Tessa was lounging in the window seat, sipping red wine.

"You need to catch up, I'm on glass number three already," she crowed, her cheeks overly pink and her eyes already slightly glazed.

"Closer to six," Mrs. Dugan whispered, smiling as she slid a bowl of beef stew and French bread in front of me as I sat down on one of the empty bar stools.

"I don't think Rowdy Raine is the look Lewis wishes to convey to the traumatized parents after all they have been through," I told her with a smile and a wink. We both knew I was a happy, lovey, drunk. I was more likely to cuddle with everyone I met than to go wild.

"Boo, Bitch," Tessa objected, sticking out her tongue at me for good measure. She was definitely past glass number three.

It took at least five glasses before she was that relaxed.

"Next time... I promise," I added the promise after she gave me the stink eye for several seconds.

"I'm going to hold you to it," she slurred with a goofy, drunken grin.

"Come on dear. Let's get you to bed," Mrs. Dugan cooed, pulling a wobbly Tessa to her feet.

"Fine," she pouted as she wobbled-walked down the hall, bouncing from wall to wall. After the second time she nearly tripped them both Mrs. Dugan released her and dashed forward to open the door to the room that Tess was using.

I shook my head and dove into my stew with vigor. The women worked magic when it came to food. It made me wonder, not for the first time, if it was talent or magic. Whatever the case, it was wonderful.

Lewis slid a cup across the bar to me as I finished my stew, taking the bowl as he did and depositing it in the dishwasher. I wasn't sure why, but I found that very sexy. I knew without looking it was his blood in the cup. There was nothing else that smelled quite so good. I did my best not to drool or gulp it down like a fiend.

Keenly aware of him watching, I sipped it slowly and concentrated on not moaning.

Chapter sixty-four

Lewis

My fledgling attacked her food with vigor. The way she inhaled the food, enjoying each bite, was amazing to watch. Her face was so expressive. I could not remember ever enjoying anything as much as she seemed to enjoy a simple meal and watching had me thinking indecent thoughts. When she got to the cup of my blood, she let out an adorable, breathy moan. I was so turned on that my canines descended. I had to excuse myself before she noticed.

Once I had my urges under control, we drove to town to meet the families. Mrs. Dugan had arranged the meeting, complete with snacks. I had thought we might invite a few of the ladies in her book club, however Raine had pointed out the parents would likely not want to have the children out of their sight after getting them back. She also reminded me that we wouldn't be discussing anything the children weren't entitled to know as well and that they might have questions of their own.

She was clearly a better leader than I was. Yet until meeting her, I didn't want to lead. Now I wasn't sure what I wanted except to spend more time with her.

I shook thoughts of the pale-haired beauty from my mind as we pulled into the parking lot. Ruby, the little fire demon, tackled me as I opened the door to the vehicle, nearly dragging me down in her excitement.

"Come on. Come on. Hurry," she demanded, hoping to punctuate her words while still trying to pull me towards the door where a plump woman with rosy cheeks and the same curly red hair stood. Now that she was clean and smiling, she was even more adorable. She was small for her age and too thin. I made a mental note to have Mrs. Dugan send care packages to all the families. I'd have Natessa's niece make a list of the snacks and foods she thought the other children would enjoy.

I looked back to check on my fledgling, noticing several of the children as well as a few of the parents, I didn't know their names and felt shame at that. My excuse for that fact was being too busy. However, that would be a lie. Truth be told, I hadn't cared to. I guess, in a way, Raine was to blame. Just not in a bad way.

The meeting went well, with the majority of the parents happy with leaving Vesper, who appeared to be the sole survivor of the entire ordeal, to the fae council. The one hold out had been a woman named Mary. Her daughter Raylin was a witch-shifter of the bear variety. Mary was a witch and her husband had been a grizzly shifter. They had lived in Alaska before he died. They had moved to the area a year ago. Mary had a sister, brother-in-law, and nephew in town. Mary had wanted to have him face the Human courts.

She wasn't used to living in a supernatural town where the police's only jobs were to patrol the road into and out of town to keep any humans not turned away by the repelling spell from entering and to deal with minor crimes committed by the local teens. Anything more than that, Natessa or I handled.

Raine and I sat with her for an hour after the others left to answer her questions and listened to her concerns. The biggest of which were being able to face the accused and to speak to the judge regarding sentencing. Both of which Raine was able to understand, since she had been raised with humans and their laws. In the end, we were able to come to a compromise.

Chapter sixty-five

Raine

By the time we left the community hall, I was feeling good about the progress we made, even if the looks Lewis was throwing my way said something different entirely.

Once we returned to the beach house, I was full of energy. I needed to burn some of it off before I could relax enough to sleep. I should have been too exhausted to move. After spending so many days searching and planning, it felt odd not having anything to keep me busy.

"I'm going to change and go for a run. If you'd like, you can join me," Lewis offered, heading toward the house.

His offer surprised me. "Sure, if you don't mind?"

"I wouldn't have offered it if I did. Though if you don't think you can keep up, I understand," he said, clearly teasing.

"Oh, I know I can old man," I mocked, running toward the door.

I made it all of four steps before he swept me off my feet and into his arms." I'll show you old," he taunted, setting me back on my feet behind him and dashing into the house as I stood there grinning like a loon. I liked this Lewis very much.

He was out of sight before I made it in the door. I ran to the room I'd been using and threw my workout clothes on and darted outside. Lewis was using the arm of an Adirondack chair to stretch. He was again wearing the low-slung basketball shorts. No man had a right to look so handsome in something so ridiculous. The lean muscles in his arms rippled beneath his pale skin as he moved. He looked like a dark god as the sun painted him in a rainbow of light as the reds and golds reflected off the water.

"Are you going to stand there and stare at me or are you going to stretch so we can burn off all this nervous energy?" he asked, making me jump.

Of course, he had heard me walk out of the house. Heat flared in my face at getting caught ogling him. In lieu of an answer, I bent to touch my toes, hiding my discomfort.

We ran for almost an hour along the water, neither of us talking, but instead of being uncomfortable, it was relaxing. Nearly every minute we'd spent together, I'd spent either fighting him, hating him, or fearing for him. We'd never spent time doing anything as simple as relaxing. I found being near him when we weren't fighting to be soothing.

When we finally called it good and headed back, I felt more settled than I had since the battle with my former friend turned snake in the grass.

"Feeling better," Lewis asked as we fell into the lawn chairs in the sand where we'd started.

"Definitely," I admitted between gulps of water.

"And no cravings?" he asked as he sipped his water, not even winded.

"Just the usual."

"The usual?" he questioned.

"You know, chocolate, salty snacks, and such. Why do you ask?"

"I was thinking about how well you are adjusting to the change. If you wanted to go home, it would probably be alright," he stated.

"I thought we would stay here until Vesper was sentenced. I promised Raylin and her mother I'd be there with them."

"Not my home. Yours, Hemlock Hollow," he said, spelling it out for me.

"But... I .... Um... Why?"

"I thought this would make you happy. I thought you wanted to see your mates," he explained, not meeting my eyes.

"I did. I mean I do. But..."

"But what?" he asked, finally looking at me.

I didn't know when that had stopped being the case, but it had. I still missed Liam and Lucian terribly, yet the idea of leaving Lewis tore at something inside me.

Chapter sixty-six

Lewis

She was quiet for so long I nearly repeated the question. However, when tears leaked from her eyes, my heart stuttered in my chest. The very thought of sending her away was tearing me up inside. But it was clear she no longer needed me. Her emotions had stayed within her control through everything, including my capture. Hell, the woman had saved us all. Clearly, she didn't need her maker around to control her. She didn't need me.

So, it was clearly time to let her go, no matter how much it hurt. The sooner I did, the sooner I could get back to normal.

"Is that what you want?" she demanded, crossing her arms and pushing her full breasts up in her already full to capacity sports bra.

"I'm sorry?" I asked. Of course, me staring at my feet in an attempt to keep from ogling her only pissed her off.

"I know you heard me. You may be older than dirt, but I know your vampire hearing works just fine," she seethed, staring me down.

Hell, the woman was tapping her sneaker clad foot while scolding me. If sending her away wasn't so hard to do, I'd have found her behavior rather entertaining. But since making her angry was the best way to distance myself from her, I leaned into her belief that I wanted her to go. I didn't. I wanted to keep her all to myself. To lock us away from everything and everyone. But I couldn't. Nor would I do that to her and her mates. To have a mate as pure and bright as Raine and lose them would be pure hell. They had entrusted me with something more precious than anything I'd come across in all my years.

"The deal was to get you through the transition. You have transitioned, job complete."

"Fine! I'll get out of your hair," she fumed, marching toward the house without looking back.

I wanted to run after her and beg her to stay. Tell her how good I wanted to be for her. But I couldn't. I may have watched over her to keep her from doing something she would regret, but I'd never had that. Discovering it was all because my brother wanted the crown didn't change the years of blood on my hands. She deserved only the best in her life. I was not that.

It took longer than I care to admit before I was in control enough to follow after her. Opening a portal for her was the least I could do since I didn't have a need for transport charms and Natessa, who did have them, was spending the night enjoying the return of her niece.

I knew as soon as I walked in; she was gone. The house felt empty and as did I.

Chapter sixty-seven

Raine

My feet carried me from the beach into the house. To think I had once thought it was a dream house. I guess it still was if nightmares counted. Once inside, I ran to the room I had used and dug through the discarded clothes until I found the transport charm Tessa had given me. As soon as I found it, I squeezed the glass vial until it broke, activating the spell. I didn't bother worrying about any of the things I'd collect in my time with Lewis. I thought of home as the shards of glass sliced my palm. The cosmos tumbled me through time and space. In a matter of moments, I landed on the porch of Hemlock House. Which is where Liam and Lucian found me. Curled on my side with tears streaming down my face and blood dripping from my hand.

Liam scooped me up from where I landed while Lucian growled something, as he did and opened the door as Reggie and Meg both fussed while Liam carried me to my old room. They had replaced my queen bed with a huge one. The new frame was real wood. It was pale with rough cut planks forming a beautiful mosaic as it climbed the wall behind the bed.

Liam must have noticed me looking because as he sat me on the edge of the new bed while Lucian bent to remove my shoes and socks, "We were going a bit stir-crazy while you were gone so Lucian came up with the idea to claim the house as ours."

"But Liam thought a bed that we could all sleep in was the best place to start," Lucian finished for him, making me want to smile. I managed a small twitch of my lips, but it felt brittle and foreign.

"It's beautiful," I told them sincerely.

"We enjoyed making it," Liam told me as he helped me out of my sports bra.

"We thought you'd enjoy being held by both of us at the same time," Lucian told me, sliding my shorts and panties down, kissing first one of my hips, then the other. Before lifting me off the bed, long enough for Liam to pull back the blanket and sheets so Lucian could place me under them.

Once I was covered up, they each lay on either side of me. I wanted to object to them, placing the blanket and sheet between them and my naked skin. I'd had dreams about them both in my bed at the same time, but my eyes were drifting shut and I'm pretty sure I was snoring, if the giggles that followed me into the land of dreams were any indication. Lucky for them both, I was too comfortable and warm to hold grudges.

When I finally woke up, sunlight was streaming through the fluttering curtains as the early spring breeze filled the room with fresh spring air. I could smell lilacs and Easter lilies, along with the fresh cut lumber scent that had filled the halls, as Liam and Lucian carried me to our bed. Both of them were absent from the bed, but I could smell both the pine and moss as well as ozone and summer rain telling me both had checked on me frequently as I slept.

That helped with the pain in my chest because of the Lewis sized hole in my heart. I stretched my stiff back and legs as I worked on convincing myself to get up and get on with my life. It took longer than I care to admit, but knowing my mates were going to want answers about how I returned helped.

I got up and headed for the shower, contemplating the merits of distracting my mates with sex to avoid that conversation for as long as possible.

Chapter sixty-eight

Lewis

As soon as I realized she was gone, I dialed Lucian Arcane. The wolf did not scare me, yet admitting his anger was justified wasn't easy, either. The one thing he asked of me was to protect her. I hadn't realized I needed to protect my heart from her. She had been gone less than half an hour and already I wanted to portal to Hemlock House and tell her how sorry I was and beg her to forgive me and never let her forget how much I truly cared.

"Hello," he answered cautiously.

"Lucian, this is Lewis Damon. Raine should be there any minute if she isn't already," I told him without preamble.

A growl that shouldn't have been possible with a human vocal cord was all I heard as he hung up unceremoniously.

I didn't know what I was going to do with my time now that she was gone. The thought of returning to my personal realm had always been soothing, a type of solace. Now it only left me feeling empty.

So, I did what any mature person would do. I threw myself into all the tasks I normally delegated to Natessa and Lily. Yet still, every day was eternal. My thoughts were constantly drifting back to her. Not since my change had I had so little control over my thoughts.

By day three I was tired, irritable, and all together unpleasant.

Which is why when Natessa appeared in the doorway of my office, I should have walked away. Of the few people in my life I'm close to, she is the one I've known the longest. She was the one who found me after I was changed. The one who helped me learn to control my blood lust.

"What the hell did you do, Lewis? She hasn't come out of her room since she left here. She hardly eats, and she refuses to see any of us. Lucian said you called and told him to look for her, and hung up without explaining. They found her in a bawling heap on the porch," she ranted.

"That is none of your business, Natessa," I told her tersely.

"On that, you would be mistaken. I care about you, and I love Raine. She has been through hell and back, she deserves happiness and honestly so have you, so I thought you of all people would understand," she seethed, slamming her hands on her hips.

"I repeat. It. Is. None. Of. Your. Business," I barked, emphasizing each word.

WARRIOR

"So that's it? You're just going to let one of the best things to ever happen to you get away?" she asked as I walked away.

I had to admit, if only to myself, that I missed her deeply.

Chapter sixty-nine

Raine

It had been four days since Lewis had sent me away. I was lying in bed rewatching old episodes of Gilmore Girls. It was my cheer up series of choice. I dare anyone to watch Lorelai Gilmore's *monkey, monkey underpants* scene and keep a straight face. I remember growing up wishing I had a mother like her.

"Hellcat, you awake?" Liam called as he tapped on the door before entering.

He was carrying a tray with food and blood. I could smell it as soon as he opened the door. Despite my inability to tolerate it, I was still unable to provide more than a brief explanation, resulting in me discreetly flushing it down the toilet when no one was around. I hadn't explained the whole chimera thing, nor the possibility that the only blood I could ingest without vomiting was my maker's. I had tried, but just like the bag blood, it tasted like feet and ass. Now logically I knew I should at least tell my mates that, but I hadn't been quite ready.

"Yeah."

He kissed my nose as he positioned the tray with the food and blood on it.

I had no appetite, however; I didn't want him to worry about me. Though when Lucian joined us, I could tell from the looks they were both giving me the time for avoidance had passed, which could only mean one of two things, either Lewis had finally answered his phone, I'd heard Lucian calling and cursing him out on what I could only assume was voicemail, or more likely that Tessa had called.

I knew she would never tell them anything she thought would hurt my trust in her, but she was not beyond telling them they should talk to me for my own good.

"I'm guessing it's answer time?" I asked, abandoning the pretense of eating.

"You know we only want to help, right, Hellcat?" Liam asked, reaching for my hand.

"And if that means we need to kill someone, you know we will," Lucian added, lacing his fingers through mine and kissing my knuckles.

"Thank you both. I'm sure it has been hard for both of you waiting for an explanation, but I appreciate it more than you know," I told them earnestly, leaning over to give first one, then the other, a kiss. Then I launched into what had happened after my brief visit with them all the way through what went down with Lewis and his brother, complete with the revelation that I was a chimera. Though I still wasn't fully sure what that was or what it meant as far as being a vampire or not. All worries for another time.

"I will be there when he is sentenced. I promised the children and their families no matter what."

"We would never ask you to go back on a promise," Lucian reassured me.

"Never, Hellcat. In fact, if you don't mind, I think Lucian and I would like to be there with you. To show our support and to meet the children you helped save," Liam added, tucking me into the crook of his arm.

I snuggled into his chest before answering, "I think I'd like that very much," I admitted.

Liam ran his fingers gently through my hair. Lucian lay against my other side, still holding my hand.

We stayed like that for quite a while, each of us enjoying the comfortable silence. The chance to just be together.

"You told us what Vesper did to Lewis, his father, and the children. What you haven't told us is what upset you so much?" Lucian pointed out.

"And if you don't want to tell us, you don't have to. But if you wanted to, we're here," Liam added, kissing the top of my head.

I had nearly forgotten how supportive they both could be. Even if Lucian's support was generally in the form of bodily injuries on my behalf.

Chapter seventy

Raine

As difficult as it was to admit, Lewis not wanting me hurt, I hadn't gone into the whole thing planning to fall for him. Just like I hadn't planned to fall for Lucian. But I had.

Lewis was unapproachable, surly, and came off as cold and uncaring. However, he was also fiercely protective, loyal, and had a heart of gold under all his many layers. Way under, but it was there.

"I guess I thought there was something where there wasn't," I finally admitted.

"Then it is his loss," Lucian growled, kissing me fiercely.

By the time he pulled away, I was panting. Liam kissed a trail of sucking, nibbling kisses along my jawline. I focused only on the path of his lips and the pleasure that trailed behind. His tongue darted out, licking a delicate line along my neck, and my head spun as heat shot to my core.

Lucian slid my night shirt up, blazing a heated trail of pleasure as his rough, callused hands stroked along my inner thigh, teasing over the lace of my panties as his mouth kissed my navel. Then the underside of each breast. His tongue flicked across my taunt nipple. While his thumb grazed across my throbbing clit. I moaned, arching into his touch.

I snaked my hand down the front of Liam's boxers, and I used my other to slide my soaking panties aside removing the barrier and begging him to touch me as I gripped Liam's shaft pumping slowly as he bucked his hips in time to my strokes.

"Damn Hellcat..." Liam hissed, sliding his boxers off, giving me an unobstructed view of his impressive length.

I wrapped my lips around the tip, tasting his seed as I took more of him into my mouth. Lucian moved his mouth to my left breast, sucking deeply while his long fingers stroked my throbbing channel, causing me to moan, the sound muffled by Liam's cock in my mouth.

Lucian made his way from my breasts to my pussy with nips and caresses. He finally buried his face in my pussy, alternating his attention between sucking my clit, running his tongue up and down my slit, and plundering my opening with his talented tongue and fingers. My legs clamped around his head as I bucked, my pleasure building with every lick and suck. I crashed over that orgasmic cliff as Lucian added a third finger to my clenching vagina.

Waves of pleasure were still wracking my body as he flipped me onto my hands and knees. Liam fucked my mouth as Lucian sank into my still pulsing channel. My walls clenched around his thick member, dancing that line between pleasure and pain. He pumped slowly, allowing me time to adjust, but that wasn't what I wanted. I wanted all of him.

I pushed back, taking him deeper. Slamming into another climax within a matter of strokes.

Multiple orgasms later, I was adrift in a sea of sexual bliss. Which is likely why I agreed to have the girls over without thinking about the third degree I knew I'd suffer. Or possibly I knew I needed their take on the whole situation, or maybe I knew they wouldn't pull any punches to spare my feelings. That wasn't what our group was about.

"SO, YOU AND TESSA TOOK on countless fae to save his ass, and he responded by sending you home?" Becca asked.

"Yeah, pretty much," I admitted.

"Boo! I saw that story going a totally different direction," Olivia admitted, refilling her wineglass then topping mine off.

Not that I needed it. We were six bottles in, and I was well and truly drunk.

"Same," Becca agreed, "But it sure sounds like there's more to the story. Maybe he was worried about you, but you proved yourself. Maybe he knew you were missing your mates and was trying to do something nice," she suggested.

"There is more," Tessa told us, speaking for the first time on the matter.

"Well then, spill bitch," Becca told her.

"I doubt Lewis ever told you about his transition, did he?" Tessa asked, ignoring Becca's comment.

"Only that it was painful, and of course we know now that it was an attempt on his life by his piece of shit brother."

"Of course he didn't," she grumbled. "Well, I'm not going to tell you anything that isn't common knowledge. However, there is a great deal more that isn't, nor is it mine to tell," she explained.

Once I gave a nod to acknowledge her statement, she continued, "You now know he wasn't meant to transition but to die on that night. While your transition was painful, Lewis was there and when he wasn't, he had Lily sit with you. Did you know that?"

"No," I admitted, but it did make sense when I thought back to when I had woken up. I could smell them both strongly in the room.

"Do you know why?" she asked.

"Not really," I admitted sheepishly. Somehow ashamed yet unsure why.

"Because he woke up alone in an alley. The vampires Vesper hired attacked while they were cutting through an alley when they got jumped. At some point, his attacker punched him in the mouth and cut himself on Lewis' teeth. He ingested a few drops of the vampire's blood when it happened. His throat was ripped out moments later. Three days later he woke bloody, hungry and sporting what he thought was a major concussion," Tessa told us.

"Then what happened?" I asked in a whisper.

"That is where my part of the story has to end. The rest you'll need to ask him about," she told me, climbing to her feet.

"What if he won't tell me?"

"Make him," she told me, leaning down to give me a quick hug. "Now, as much as I hate to drink and run, I have court in the morning and a hung-over lawyer isn't a good look."

Chapter seventy-one

Raine

Not long after Tessa left, the party broke up. Paul picked up Becca, and Olivia crashed into one of the spare rooms. Bethany was newly mated to Lucian's brother Roman Arcane, who was the alpha of the Illinois Basin pack, so she hadn't been able to get away on such short notice with all her new duties.

Once Olivia had settled in for the night, I changed into a bathing suit and headed to the hot tub. Lucian had installed it out back while I was gone as a mating gift. I decided it was a pastime to try it out.

I had just settled in to enjoy the view of the forest behind the house when Liam came out of the house. He didn't get in with me, but he sat on the edge, rolled up his pant legs and pulled me closer so he could rub my neck and shoulders.

"Did you ladies have a good time?" He asked.

"Yeah, it was nice. Even though Tessa was helping with the search, it most certainly wasn't relaxing in the least. Tonight, we laughed, we drank too much wine and caught up. I'm glad they came."

"So, no boy bashing?" he teased. "I thought that's what women did when they got together."

"No, that's just what men like to think we do," I joked.

"Oh, I see. You got jokes, huh?" he mocked, tickling me.

I splashed him and I darted across the hot tub to the other side. He splashed back, and it turned into a water fight with me finally pulling him in jeans and all. By the time it was over, I was laughing so hard I had tears leaking from my eyes.

"I missed you so much, Hellcat. I'm really happy you are back," he told me, helping me out of the warm water and wrapped a towel around me.

"I missed you too, and it's good to be home," I told him, hugging him tightly.

"That's because I'm a wonderful mate," he joked.

"You are very modest," I mocked with a sappy smile.

"For what it's worth, Hellcat, I don't think he meant to hurt you," Liam offered as we made our way toward the house.

"Then why did he send me away without even asking what I wanted or how I felt about it?"

"I'm sure he thought it was better for you to come home, safer maybe, since you don't know for sure all the dark witches and such that were working with his brother are gone. Or if being a chimera will make you a bigger target," Liam offered.

"I am not some delicate flower. I know how to protect myself."

"No, love, you most definitely are not. You are deadly, just like the town you were born to rule," Liam told me, leaning his forehead against mine. From anyone else, that line might have sounded cheesy. But to me it was pure sweetness, just like him.

Standing there in Liam's arms, I thanked the powers of the universe for bringing him to my life.

Chapter seventy-two

Raine

The day of the sentencing I was up at four in the morning with hours to kill until we would need to leave. For the first time since discovering I was a witch, I was sorry that the travel time was minutes with a transport charm instead of driving for hours. At least, then I would have something to do with my time.

Since I didn't, I was in the workshop making use of the time by making healing potions and restocking the transport charms. Apparently, they had needed many of both while I was gone. I was going to need to ask what all transpired while I had been away. The thought left me feeling very selfish for making my return all about what had happened to me. I'd left Lucian less than a day after our mating, and Liam and I had only weeks together.

"I can see you overthinking things from here," Lucian told me from the doorway.

Since he wasn't wrong, and I wasn't willing to admit anything, I just stuck my tongue out at him and continued corking the potion vials.

"Liam said you wanted to leave in thirty minutes, so here's your thirty-minute warning," he told me.

"Five minutes and I'll be ready. Just restocking healing potions and transport charms. Seems like a great deal of them were needed while I was gone."

"Other than Tessa's friend getting shot, not really. However, Liam and I have been delivering them to families that don't reside in Hemlock. We figured not everyone would be able to get here for healing and the charms have been mainly used for Tessa, Becca, and Bethany to travel to and from seeing their men," he explained with a chuckle.

"I like the idea of making sure our people all have access to healing. Now on to the juicy part of that disclosure. Obviously, I know Bethany is with Roman, but who are Becca and Tessa's men? I feel so behind."

"If you are good, I promise to tell you all the things you missed," he told me, kissing.

As much fun as it would have been to enjoy where his kisses could lead, I needed to change before we left. I had promised to meet anyone who wished to attend at the town hall, mainly to avoid Lewis, so I could transport them to Fairie for the sentencing.

Ruby, Raylin, Markus and their parents were waiting when we arrived in Damon Cove. Ruby nearly bowled me over as I stepped through the portal charm.

"Raine! You're here!" she yelled, hugging me tightly with her little arms.

Her volume was uncomfortable for my sensitive ears, but I smiled and hugged her back. I was happy to see she looked healthy after all she'd been through.

"I am," I agreed, placing her back on her feet as her mother joined us.

"She has told everyone how you and Mr. Damon saved her and her friends," her mother told me.

"Who are you?" Ruby asked Lucian, staring up at him.

"Ruby, manners," her mother scolded.

Lucian squatted down to her level smiling, "It's alright. My name is Lucian Arcane. I'm one of Raine's mates."

Markus and his father both dropped to one knee and exposed their necks to Lucian. He bowed his head in acknowledgement.

"You're a wolf?" Ruby asked in awe.

"I am," Lucian told her with a smile before scenting the air, "And you are a fire-demon."

"Yep," she told him, smiling. "Are you Ms. Raine's mate too?" she asked Liam craning her neck to see him.

"I am. My name is Liam," he told her.

"You're really tall. Are you a wolf too?" she blurted.

"Yes, I am tall, but no, I'm not a wolf. I'm her witch mate," Liam explained.

"Cool," she told him, drawing out the word and making everyone laugh.

Once everyone was ready, I dropped the charm and envisioned the king's castle in Fairie.

Chapter seventy-three

Lewis

I did my best to keep my thoughts away from the pale-haired vixen that had haunted my dreams since I had sent her home, or she ran away. Depending on how you looked at it. Either way, she was gone and some part of me felt like all the light was gone from my world. Hell, maybe there never was any until she came along.

Natessa and Lily kicked me for letting Raine go, and I kicked myself for falling for her, leaving my emotions battered and bruised. Every beat of my undead heart was misery.

Mrs. Dugan had received calls from the parents that wanted to attend Vesper's trail, informing me that my portal services would not be needed. Apparently, even my citizens loved her.

Lily and Hector had opted not to attend, and Natessa was transporting with her brother Theirry and her niece Suma. I still prefer that the children not attend. Yet another thing I was not a fan of.

I waited until the last minute to open a portal to the throne room. My father no longer used it since his office was more practical. Since Vesper's sentencing was open to the public, again thanks to my fledgling, the proceedings were taking place in the great hall to accommodate everyone. The fact she was a rare, one of a kind being likely had a great deal to do with his agreement.

I slid into the hall and stayed in the back of the room. I still wasn't sure how I was supposed to feel about all my brother had done. I knew he was jealous, but never thought it would lead to half the things he had done for power. Especially since power was never something I craved.

When my brother was led into the hall in shackles, I felt like a part of me should stand up for him. Like maybe this was all a nightmare. The brother I thought I knew made stupid mistakes but would never purposely hurt people and definitely never children. Once he was seated at the front of the room, the long list of charges was read. The list was longer than even I knew.

"How ya doing?" Natessa inquired, standing next to where I leaned against the rear wall.

"I'm not sure, honestly," I admitted. Natessa was one of the few people I could be that honest with without feeling like she might exploit it. Lily was the other.

"I think that's normal," she assured me.

The boy, Walter, whose powers Vesper drained, was standing in front of the council as they asked him questions. He was the first, but he stood tall and answered each question without getting emotional. That wasn't the case with the majority of the people who spoke against my brother.

The proceedings seemed to both go on forever and pass by in a moment simultaneously. When the council stepped out to confer, the hall containing over one hundred observers remained silent, collective breaths held as they awaited Vesper's fate.

The assembly filed back in, taking their seats. Normally, father sat as head of the council, however today he was not acting in that capacity, but he still sat in his seat of power.

"Vesper Tuatha de Dannan rise, you will now face judgment for the crimes you have been found guilty of," the elder member of the council commanded.

When my brother did not stand as directed, the guards on either side of him pulled him to his feet.

"For your numerous crimes against not only your people, innocent children, but your king, you will be stripped of your powers, your titles, and will be cast out of the fae lands. You will not return or interact with any of the citizens of this land for no less than one hundred years," he decreed in a booming voice.

There were several astonished gasps from the spectators. Thene there was a commotion near the front of the space, but I'd seen what I came for. The rest I had no desire to be present for. The pain that Vesper would endure during the stripping of his powers would be severe, but even without his gifts, his life span would be the same as without them. Though without them, he could be injured or even killed with the right implement. Which was something I didn't care to think about.

My hand was on the door to leave when I heard her voice. I was turned around and striding towards her before the thought had formed.

"King Tuatha de Dannan," Raine called. Her dulcet tones danced across my senses as I fought the crush of onlookers trying to reach the beauty that had plagued my every thought since her departure.

I pushed forward, moving as swiftly as the crowd would allow, but when I reached the dais, neither my fledgling nor my father were anywhere to be seen. I searched for several minutes, even looking for her mates when I was unable to locate her. There was no sign of them.

I'd finally given up searching and had turned to slink away, possibly even working up the nerve to call her, when a tug on my hand had me looking down into a pair of piercing green eyes.

"Where ya going?" Ruby asked me, her southern drawl was very pronounced.

"Oh, hello Ruby, how are you?"

"Fine. What ya doin?" she inquired.

"Ruby, please leave Mr. Damon alone and get over here so we can go," called a slight woman with the same crimson hair and emerald eyes as the little girl.

"Bye," the little girl told me with a wave as she skipped away.

I smiled despite my poor mood and followed in her wake as I made my way toward the throne room to portal home, still thinking about Raine. I'd spoken to her first mate four times in the past week just to be sure she was adjusting well. That she wasn't having mood swings or outbursts. He did little more than answer my questions with *yes* and *no* answers. It was enough that I knew she wasn't at risk of harming anyone. Or at least that was what I told myself.

Chapter seventy-four

Raine

Vesper's sentence wasn't what I had hoped for, not fully. The only thing that would keep him from hurting others again was a death sentence, however having his magic stripped had given me an idea. Which was why I was attempting to convince Lewis' father to let me strip his son's magic so I could try to give Walter back the power that was stolen from him.

"So, you wish to attempt something on my son that you have merely *read* about, so you may endeavor to give the fae child back the power that was taken from him? Is that correct?" Lewis' father summarized.

I'd done a fair bit more than *read* about it, but to be diplomatic, I agreed.

"Basically."

"And what will happen if this does not go as planned, as they say?" he questioned.

"If you are asking, if it will kill him. The answer is no. Though I'm not going to promise it wouldn't be painful. In fact, I think a bit of pain is the least Vesper should suffer after all the people he has hurt," I admitted bluntly.

"And the boy?" he inquired.

"He isn't in danger. Nor will he experience any type of pain."

"Have you spoken to the boy's parents?" he questioned.

"Not yet. I did not want to get their hopes up before speaking to you."

"That is wise. I have to say I was not expecting this to be what you wished to speak to me in relation to. If I were you, I would want to know everything I could about what I was," he stated.

"She is not you father. She always thinks of others before herself," I heard Lewis telling his father.

I whipped around to see him standing in the doorway to his father's office.

"Yes, Luwianos, it is quite clear she is something altogether unique. What are your thoughts on her request?" Lewis' father asked him.

"And what request would that be?" Lewis questioned, his eyes locked on mine.

"She would like to extract Vesper's magic and dissect out the magic he took from the fae boy and return it to him" he explained.

"I think if she says she can do it, I'd believe her," he remarked, surprising me.

Several uncomfortable moments passed in silence before his father told me, "If the parents are agreeable to this, I see no reason I should not allow it."

"Perfect, thank you. I'll go ask them right now," I told him, turning to leave and to put some distance between myself and my sire.

I took off like my ass was on fire, putting distance between me and the man and the feelings he ignited. However, I had no clue where I was going, and I had left so quickly I'd lost not just one of my mates but both of them.

I don't know how long I was wandering before I heard the sound of walking coming from one of the rooms. Since the hall I found myself in seemed to be rarely used, I took my chances and followed the sound until I reached the throne room. Naturally, the person I found was the last one I wanted to see.

Of all the people and all the places in a castle large enough to house one hundred people, it had to be him. Lewis was pacing the area in front of his father's throne, muttering to himself.

"What the hell was I thinking? Why didn't I keep my mouth shut? But no, I have to open my mouth and send her running in the opposite direction. Maybe in a few hundred years she will forget how much of an asshat I have been," he ranted.

I backed away slowly, intent on finding someone else. Anyone else. My footsteps must have betrayed my presence because he ceased muttering.

"Raine-," he started.

"I didn't mean to interrupt. I'll just be on my way so you can get back to... it," I told him, darting away before he could say more.

"Wait," he called as I sprinted away.

Chapter seventy-five

Lewis

The sound of a shoe scuffing across the floor alerted me to my visitor. Raine was the last person I expected to see when I looked up. I could hardly believe my luck at seeing her there, but she was gone faster than virginity at a frat party.

So, as dumb as I knew it was, I chased her through the castle and onto the front lawn, where several people were still milling about. I caught up to her when she was still ten feet away from the closest person.

"Please Raine, can we go somewhere and talk?" I pleaded with her.

"No," she grunted.

"Please," I tried again.

She crossed her arms under her breast and demanded, "Fine, talk!"

"I was hoping for someplace a little more private."

"Yeah, and I was hoping you'd fuck off, but apparently neither of us is getting what we hoped for now, are we?" she growled, tapping her foot impatiently.

I'm not going to say I didn't think about letting her walk away and waiting those hundred plus years to tell her how I felt but I knew if I didn't try, I was going to live every one of those days in complete and utter misery. So, I swallowed my fear and pride and spoke my truth, as they say.

"For some reason I can't identify, I feel an overwhelming need to protect you. My heart views you as mine. I cannot pinpoint when this need took hold, just that it continues to grow stronger the longer I'm near you. You are constantly on my mind. I crave you. I dream of you. When I haven't dreamt in, I don't know how long. Yet I am powerless to absolve my desire for you," Lewis declared.

"Is that all you feel for me is desire?" she asked quietly.

"No, of course not."

"Then why push me away?" she wanted to know.

"For the same reason, I wanted to shelter you during your transition, so you didn't have to suffer with the memory of all those you'd hurt during your blood lust. As I do," I admitted.

She moved closer, and I reached up to stroke her face gently. I pulled my hand away, but she leaned into my touch and something inside me sang at this small measure of acceptance.

"Then stop acting like the man you think you are. Be the man I know you have become," she commanded.

"You make it sound so simple."

"Nothing worth having has ever been simple," she told me.

She searched my face as she waited for a reply. Truthfully, I wanted her more than I'd ever wanted anything. "

"I can't promise to be perfect, but I will promise to always try my best."

"That's all I ask," she countered, her smirk the best thing I'd seen in all my years.

As I stood there smiling like a love-struck teen, all I wanted was to take her in my arms and kiss her senseless.

"Are you two good now?" Natessa asked as she joined us.

"I believe we are well on our way," Raine admitted.

"Good, then let's get out of here and do something fun," Natessa suggested.

"As much as I would like that, I have something I need to do. Rain check?" Raine offered.

"Fine," Natessa pouted, "But you better bet I'm going to hold you to it, bitch. Don't make me go all psycho-bitch on you, woman. You know I will."

"Yeah, I'm aware," Raine told her with a warm smile and a tight hug.

"Hellcat, there you are," Liam told his mate as he joined us.

"Did you find Walter and Williamina's parents?" she asked by way of response as he kissed her cheek softly.

"They are waiting for us over there," he told her, pointing off to the right where I could see her second mate Lucian standing.

"Okay, great," she replied, turning to me." I'm sorry I know there's more to talk about, but I need to talk to Walter's family before they leave."

"Of course, I understand."

"Unless... Do you want to come with me? I mean, you don't have to, but if you want, we could talk more when I'm done," she offered.

Chapter seventy-six

Raine

I couldn't believe Lewis had said the things he had, and I knew we had plenty more to discuss and work through, but being near him felt right. Like getting back the use of a limb I never knew was missing. Which is why we were now back at his home in Damon Cove, setting things up to return Walter's power. Thankfully, the fae mean business when they sentence a criminal. Vesper's power was removed with the use of blue sapphire and amethyst cuffs I'd spent six hours creating. The magic he was born with flows through the gemstone cuffs and returns to the Fae realm while absorbing the stolen magic. Then the cuffs were placed on Walter, at which time I would draw the remaining magic through him. If it worked, the power that belonged to him would remain, whereas the rest would be released and neutralized.

Walter and Williamina arrived with their parents promptly at eleven-thirty, as I'd instructed. The twins were miniature copies of their parents, from the cinnamon brown eyes to the chestnut curls and button nose.

They stood around the circle of salt I'd set up before they arrived. I'd explained what to expect before I let them agree. Everything pointed to it working and not causing the boy any discomfort. Still, I told Walter again and watched both his face and his parents looking for signs of doubt or fear. When I did not find it, I walked into the ring of salt and closed the circle by spreading salt across the opening I'd left.

Walter and I sat facing each other, and I lit the white taper candles at the four points of the compass. I placed the cuffs on Walter and gave his hand a reassuring pat before beginning. The spell required no words, only intentions. I had visualized it down to an art, thanks to Liam's grandmother, who made it her mission to ensure nothing could break my focus by doing anything and everything she could imagine distracting me. It took no time at all for me to find the strand of my power I'd used to tie the stolen magic from Vesper to the stones. There were actually four strands of magic that hadn't belonged to him. Two were fresh and bright, leading me to believe they were fae powers. The other two were dark and nasty, so they would be neutralized as they passed out of the circle of protection where we sat.

I tugged the strand of magic, allowing it to unravel slowly as I directed it from the cuffs through Walter. The first was one of the dark powers and, other than a frown, Walter showed no reaction. The second was one of the strands that smelled of grass and green apples. I got excited as the magic coated the boy. He smiled and his skin glowed for a moment, but then lifted from his skin and blew away with the cool night air. Power number three smelled of sulfur and heat as it passed from the cuff and into the ground. I crossed everything I could as power number four crawled slowly from the cuffs and Walter's skin briefly glowed with a sea-green light before absorbing and disappearing.

We all held our breath as Waler opened his eyes and smiled.

"Did it work?" his sister demanded, startling me.

In answer, Walter shot a stream of water from his hand into the air, showering everyone with a fine mist of water. Walter and his sister laughed as she tackle-hugged him. They rolled around laughing and wrestling for a few minutes and I couldn't have been happier. As someone who had mourned the possible loss of my witch and wolf powers, I understood the joy he felt.

Once Walter and his family left, I was suddenly nervous about being alone with Lewis when it was all I'd wanted when he sent me away. We were sitting on the deck behind the house. The full moon reflecting off the waves of the ocean. The briny air was warm and refreshing like Illinois' weather never seemed to be.

"I can see that brain of yours thinking. Anything you'd like to share?" Lewis asked, smiling in a teasing fashion.

"Not thinking as much as worrying," I admitted.

"About?" he inquired.

I took several minutes to organize my thoughts so I could explain. Once I had, I turned in the chair, so I faced him and gave as honest an answer as possible.

"I know you didn't want a fledgling, but I can't be sad that it was you or even that I died because it brought me to you. But I'm not going to lie to you. You sending me away hurt."

"I am aware that it did. I'm sorry. It was never my intention to cause you pain; In fact, I wanted to save you from the guilt I had to suffer. That I still suffer with. You deserve better. That is why I sent you away even though it broke something inside me," he told me with his eyes pleading for me to understand.

He ran his thumb across my bottom lip where I had been chewing it, trying to keep the tears from my eyes as I thought of the loneliness he must have suffered all those years. His touch was so soft, so reverent, daring me to deny him. Not that I could have. The pain and fear in his eyes made my soul ache for all that he had suffered.

Lewis' head dipped low, and I tensed in anticipation of his mouth touching mine. But he only paused, hovering there, eyes searching. "Do you want me to kiss you?" he whispered.

"I want you to do more than that," I replied honestly. Just the idea of it sent heat pooling low in my belly.

His eyes glittered with delicious mischief.

"I want to kiss you in places no one has ever kissed you," he told me.

My nipples hardened at the mere suggestion. As if he could read my mind, his hand landed on my hip, and he pulled me closer. Holy hell! The moment I'd been waiting for had arrived.

Chapter seventy-seven

Lewis

Raine's lips were full and soft as I sucked and nibbled on her lower lip. Teasing and sucking until she was moaning with each stroke of my tongue. I pulled her into my arms, cupped her full ass, lifted her, and wrapped her legs around my waist as I pinned her to the glass patio doors. My cock was hard enough to cut glass as I ground against her core. She bucked against me, threading her fingers in my hair and tugging my mouth to her pert breast. I pulled back long enough to remove her shirt, exposing her black lace bra underneath. I sucked her taut nipple through the lace as I reached behind her to undo the clasp.

I removed it and sucked one breast while pinching the stiff peak of the other. She reached between us, sliding her hand down the front of my trousers and stroked my length. I followed her lead and undid her zipper, snaking my free hand down her jeans and stroking her until she screamed her release, grinding against me as she rode my finger to a second orgasm.

Her deft strokes had me ready to explode like a randy teen in no time. Since I did not wish to embarrass myself, nor was I ready to call it a night with my fair-haired temptress. I slid her down the wall until her feet were touching long enough to strip her jeans and panties off.

Turning her away from me and placing her hands against the sliding doors, bending her at the waist and spreading her legs as wide as possible. Running my hands slowly down her ass, I knelt behind her and buried my face in her pussy, tasting all of her. I sucked her clit, and she pushed her core into my face as I slid two fingers inside her, tilting her ass so I could tease her back entrance with my thumb. She was dripping wet as she screamed my name when she climaxed a third time.

Unable to hold back any longer, I stood behind her and slid into her, slamming my hips into her as I held her hips firmly. Reaching around to stroke that bundle of nerves as I took her fast and hard. I pulled out and pulled Raine with me, turning her as I sat on the chair I had vacated. I guided her to straddle me so I could see her beautiful face as I made love to her.

She rode me until we both came screaming the others' names. We were both panting as she lay on my chest. Her skin glowed in the light of the full moon.

"You are so beautiful."

"You're not so bad yourself," she smirked, kissing the tip of my nose before climbing to her feet and walking off the deck, heading toward the ocean.

"Where are you going?"

"For a swim. Care to join me?" she asked, shaking her ass in my direction before dashing into the water.

We swam, splashed, and made love until the sun came up when we fell asleep in each other's arms. I'd never in my life felt the peace and rightness that I did laying with her in my arms watching her sleep.

As I laid there watching her, I made a list of the things I would need to do to transition Lily into the leadership role. I'd always planned to pass the mantel to her. Natessa would draw up the appropriate paperwork and what not.

When I heard Mrs. Dugan speaking with someone in the kitchen, I slid her hand from my chest in an attempt to let her sleep. My plan to let her sleep was unsuccessful.

"Change your mind?" she asked.

It was clear she had wanted it to sound teasing, however. The tone fell flat, and the fear was clear in her amber eyes.

"No. Never. I heard Mrs. Dugan answer the door and let someone in. I thought it might be your mates and did not want to wake you while I went to investigate, in case it was not."

She smiled and grabbed my face, pulling my mouth to her so she could kiss me. It was little more than a soft peck, yet still my undead heart soared. I offered her a hand up and retrieved a robe for her, then slid into a pair of shorts.

We were both surprised to find my father in the kitchen sipping coffee while he sat at the table chatting with Mrs. Dugan.

"Father, is everything alright?"

"Yes, of course. I merely wanted to check in and thank Ms. Hemlock for all she has done and you as well. Without you and your people, I don't want to think of what the outcome would have been," he stated.

"I merely did what any decent person would have done," Raine offered, sipping the coffee I'd made for her.

"Oh, how I wish that were true. At any rate, we are blessed to have someone as caring and determined as you are looking out for those who can't protect themselves. If you ever need anything that I can help with, all you need to do is ask," father told her. Which surprised me because he never admitted weakness or offered aid. He most definitely did not treat others as his equal, yet that was what he did for her.

It appeared Raine had impressed even the fae king.

Chapter seventy-eight

Raine

Lewis' father stayed for over an hour chatting and offering the use of his personal library for any research I might wish to do related to my chimera genetics. I assured him that when I was ready, I would take him up on his offer. For the present, I was looking forward to returning to Hemlock Hollow and my mates.

"Would you like to talk to them without me first? I have to admit I never planned to be anyone's mate, so I did not give much attention to what or how things occurred for others who did," Lewis admitted once his father left.

"There doesn't appear to be a right or wrong way to mate," I told him. "It's merely what feels right. I would like you to be there so we can talk to Liam and Lucian together. However, if you would like me to go alone, I can."

"Then I'm ready when you are," Lewis told me with a broad smile.

He was clearly nervous, which I found to be utterly adorable. I waited several minutes for him to open a portal, when he didn't, I retrieved a transport charm and took us home.

We found Lucian and Liam in the kitchen with Meg. The guys were eating while looking over some blueprints. They both seemed to be getting into the whole renovation thing.

They both looked up as we entered the kitchen.

Lucian was up and hefting me into his arms, "Hey doll, I missed you," he bellowed, lifting me high enough to claim my mouth in a toe-curling kiss before passing me to Liam's waiting arms.

"Howdy, Hellcat. I missed you more," he told me, kissing each corner of my mouth gently before claiming my lips fully. By the time he sat me back on my feet, I was smiling from ear to ear.

"I missed you both, too. What are we looking to remodel next?" I asked, leaning over the blueprint of Hemlock House.

"Just looking for a room suitable for your newest mate. Unless, of course, we are reading the sappy smile you're wearing incorrectly," Liam started with a cheeky grin.

We all looked at Lewis, waiting for his response.

"I'd rather sleep with you, Love but if it's important for me to have my own space, I'll be happy wherever you have room," Lewis replied, taking me in his arms and nuzzling my neck.

"Yes, Romeo it is necessary because at some point the woman is going to get tired and you randy men will need somewhere to sleep," Liam's grandmother Gigi cackled, joining us in the kitchen.

I couldn't help the snicker that escaped at her bluntness. She was a fiery little thing that I loved dearly.

"Hey, Gigi. What's up?" Liam asked his grandmother, leaning down to kiss the little woman's cheek.

"Not much when you reach my age, son, but thanks for asking," she deadpanned.

"Mother!" Liam's mother Rose chastised.

"So, this is the final mate, huh?" Gigi stated, circling Lewis while looking him up and down. "Not bad to look at. Not that I've ever had a dalliance with a vampire but-"

"Mother enough!" Rose barked. "I'm so sorry."

"So am I. He's a hunk," Gigi continued, unaffected by her daughter's embarrassment. "Oh, don't get your knickers in a bunch, Rose. I'm old, not dead," she laughed, enjoying her daughter's discomfort.

Everyone, including Lewis, laughed, though Rose tried her best not to.

"Well, we came to invite you all to dinner. If you are up to it, that is," Rose offered.

"That is very kind of you. We'd love to. What time?"

We chatted about dinner and caught up with what everyone had been up to.

"Are you ready to run yet?" Lucian asked Lewis as Liam showed his mother and grandmother out.

"Not even a little," Lewis told him, wearing a wide smile as he draped his arm around my shoulder.

Epilogue

WAKING TO ALL THREE of my mates wrapped around me gave me a feeling of completeness, like nothing else I'd ever known. It had been six blissful weeks since I'd brought Lewis home. He had dived into mating headfirst. He, Lucian and Liam had settled in with utter ease and while they each were different in so many ways, they were the same in that they would do anything I asked as long as it made me happy, and they made me happy. So very happy that I'd found each one of them.

Since our mating, Lewis had begun to transition leadership of Damon Cove to Lily, with Tessa as her second. We would visit and check in, but he had always planned to relinquish his role to her, as she was the reason he had even wanted to create Damon Cove in the first place. Lily and Hector were staying in the house in Damon Cove while they waited for their new house to be built. It would be on the same property, though Lewis felt they would enjoy something all their own.

Today, however, was the official celebration and presentation of all three of my mates. While it was actually a witch thing to present the four of us as mated, I was excited for my people to meet them. I knew beyond a shadow of a doubt that each one of them would do whatever it took for our people, witch, wolf, and everyone in between.

"That is an awfully big smiling Hellcat. Care to tell me what is making you so happy already this morning?" Liam asked, stroking a hand across my bottom lip.

I nipped his finger lightly with my teeth before answering, "Just taking stock of all I have to be thankful for."

"Oh yeah? Like?" he asked, peppering my neck with gentle kisses. Making me moan.

"You, for one, my sweet witch," I replied, kissing his full lips.

"What about your favorite wolf?" Lucian asked, pulling me closer so he could claim my lips in a fiery assault of tongue and teeth that left me panting and needy.

"Of course I'm thankful for you, my fierce wolf," I told him, cuddling into his chest.

Lewis, who was lying on the other side of Liam, crawled over him and slid between him and me, nipping my shoulder lightly with his fangs, sending heat shooting to my core.

"You better not be starting something you can't finish, Mister," I told him with a smirk.

I'd quickly learned Lewis loved nothing more than a challenge. Our official bonding was in two hours, which meant the girls would be showing up any minute and I still needed to take a shower. I had moved to crawl out of bed to do exactly that when Lewis bolted from the bed and made a beeline for the bathroom. I was still admiring his bare ass when Lucian swept me up into his arms and followed Lewis with Liam, hot on our heels.

It was a very pleasurable shower, and the smile I was wearing when the girls arrived apparently said it all.

"I was really hoping I wasn't going to have to smell sex so early in the morning. I see that boat has sunk," Lucian's little sister Payton said, leaning in to hug me then punching her brother in the arm.

"Witch smelling for the win," Liam's sister Becca hailed hugging Liam, Lucian, me and then Lewis who still looked uncomfortable every time she did it, but she had warned him she was a hugger and that he was now her family too.

Bethany, Lanie, Olivia, Tessa, and Lily arrived and kicked the guys out so they could help me get ready.

Once I was deemed ready, I didn't have far to go. The front yard had been transformed with twinkling lights draped in the live oaks that lined the lane leading to the house. The Spanish moss that required GiGi's special potions to survive in Illinois gave the trees a magical quality. It was yet another reason I felt blessed to have finally found my family.

They'd used the lane to create an aisle. Then they'd used astro turf to lead to a flower arch. Lilac and rose petals were scattered up the path, which was lined with chairs that were filled with family, friends, and all manner of supernatural. Since people still believed I was a hybrid, the influx of others wishing to live in Hemlock Hollow was ever growing. Tessa had been working with a handsome witch teacher to fund more teachers and staff for the school. I was hoping it went well for both the town and maybe even for my friend. From the little Liam and Lucian had told me she seemed to like spending time with him, and from what I had learned, he was a nice guy from a well-known family. Tessa needed a nice guy. She worked too hard.

I strolled down the aisle to the three men that had become my heart. They each owned their own piece of me and without them, I would not be complete. Liam was my kindness; Lucian was my strength, and Lewis was my wisdom. They made me better and, most importantly, they made me happier than I ever thought I could be.

The End

About the author

Sandra Kaye is a registered nurse by day and an indie author by night. She was born and raised in a small town in central Illinois. In her spare time, she enjoys reading anything she can get her hands on as long as it's fiction. Writing is something she's enjoyed on and off throughout her life, while putting it into print is new. She has the support of her family, which includes an awesome man, five adult children, and four grandchildren.

Feel free to stalk me on social media.

On Facebook

Https://www.facebook.com/sandra.dawson.9235[1]

https://www.facebook.com/sandrakayeauthor13/

On Instagram

https://www.instagram.com/authorsandrakaye13/

---

1. https://www.facebook.com/sandra.dawson.9235

also by Sandra kaye

Ravenwood Series
Origins
Hunted
Hemlock Hollow
Witch
Wolf
Warrior

HTTPS://WWW.SANDRAKAYEAUTHOR.com

Don't miss out!

Visit the website below and you can sign up to receive emails whenever Sandra Kaye publishes a new book. There's no charge and no obligation.

https://books2read.com/r/B-A-UNMRB-HEHPD

BOOKS 2 READ

Connecting independent readers to independent writers.

www.ingramcontent.com/pod-product-compliance
Lightning Source LLC
Chambersburg PA
CBHW061426150726
47987CB00001B/112